Chester Himes

ALL SHOT UP

Chester Himes was born in Missouri in 1909. He began writing while serving a prison sentence for jewel theft. He published over sixty stories and just short of twenty novels before his death in 1984.

Books by Chester Himes
in the Harlem Detectives series

A Rage in Harlem

The Real Cool Killers

The Crazy Kill

All Shot Up

The Big Gold Dream

The Heat's On

Cotton Comes to Harlem

Blind Man with a Pistol

Plan B

ALL SHOT UP

ALL SHOT UP

Chester Himes

Vintage Crime/Black Lizard
VINTAGE BOOKS
A DIVISION OF PENGUIN RANDOM HOUSE LLC
NEW YORK

FIRST VINTAGE CRIME/BLACK LIZARD EDITION 2024

The Library of Congress has cataloged
the Vintage Crime/Black Lizard edition as follows:
Names: Himes, Chester B., 1909–1984, author.
Title: All shot up / Chester Himes.
Description: First Vintage Crime/Black Lizard edition. | New York :
Vintage Crime/Black Lizard, 2024.
Identifiers: LCCN 2023037075 (print) | LCCN 2023037076 (ebook)
Subjects: LCGFT: Detective and mystery fiction. | Novels.
Classification: LCC PS3515.I713 A78 2024 (print) | LCC PS3515.I713 (ebook) |
DDC 813/.54—dc23
LC record available at https://lccn.loc.gov/2023037075
LC ebook record available at https://lccn.loc.gov/2023037076

Vintage Crime/Black Lizard Trade Paperback ISBN: 978-0-593-68611-9
eBook ISBN: 978-0-593-68612-6

blacklizardcrime.com

Printed in the United States of America
10 9 8 7 6 5 4 3 2 1

ALL SHOT UP

1

It was eleven-thirty at night on ground-hog day in Harlem. It was bitter cold, and the Harlem ground hogs, as the warm-blooded Harlem citizens are called during the cold winter months, were snug in their holes.

All except one.

On the dark crosstown street off Convent Avenue, bordering the estate of the convent from which the avenue derives its name, a man was taking a wheel from a car parked in the shadow of the convent wall. He was wearing dark-brown coveralls, a woolen-lined army fatigue jacket, and a fur-lined, dark-plaid hunter's cap.

He had the inside wheel jacked up on the slanting street, making the car tilt dangerously. But he was unconcerned. He worked swiftly, without light. In the almost black dark, his face was imperceptible. At certain angles the whites of his eyes twinkled like luminous crescents stirred by the wind. His breath made pale white geysers, coming from his unseen face.

He leaned the wheel against the side of the car, lowered the axle to the pavement, glanced briefly up and down the street and began jacking up the outside wheel.

He had the wheel jacked up and the dust cap off and was fitting his wrench to a lug, when the lights of a car, turning into the street from Convent Avenue, caused him to jump back into the shadows.

The car approached and passed, not going fast, not going slow.

His eyes popped. He knew he was sober. He hadn't been drinking any whisky and he hadn't been smoking any weed. But he didn't believe what he saw. It was a mirage; but this was not the desert, and he was not dying of thirst. In fact he was cold enough for his guts to freeze; and the only thing he wanted to drink was hot rum and lemon.

He saw a Cadillac pass, the likes of which he had never seen. And his business was cars.

This Cadillac looked as though it were made of solid gold. All except the top, which was some kind of light, shining fabric. It looked big enough to cross the ocean, if it could swim. It lit up the black-dark street like a passing bonfire.

The instrument panel gave off strange blue light. It was just strong enough to illuminate the three persons occupying the front seat.

The man driving wore a coonskin Davy Crockett cap, with a big bushy tail. Beside him sat the beauty queen of Africa with eyes like frostbitten plums and a smile showing blue-dyed teeth in a black-painted skeleton's head.

The joker's heart gave a lurch. There was something shockingly familiar about that face. But it was impossible for his own true Sassafras to be riding about in a brand-new Caddy with two strange men at this hour of the night. So his gaze switched quickly to the third party, who was wearing a black Homburg and a white silk scarf and had a small, bearded face like some kind of amateur magician.

In the soft, blue-tinted light they looked like things that couldn't happen, not even in Harlem on ground-hog night.

He looked at the license of the big gold car to steady himself. It was a dealer's license. He felt a momentary reassurance. Must be a publicity gag.

All of a sudden a woman came out of nowhere. He had just time enough to see that she was an old woman dressed in solid black, her silver-white hair shining briefly in the headlights before she was hit by the golden Cadillac and knocked down.

He felt his scalp crawl and his kinky hair stand straight up beneath his fur-lined cap. He wondered if he was dreaming.

But the Cadillac took on speed. That was no dream. That was the thing to do. Just what he would have done if he had run over an old woman on a dark, deserted street.

He hadn't seen the Cadillac actually run over the old woman. But there she lay and there it went. So it must have run over her. It made sense.

Anyway, he wasn't flipping his lid. Now the question was—should he get this other wheel or should he scram with the one he had? He had an order for two. He needed the money. That little chippie he was so crazy about had told him the palm needed greasing. She didn't say palm, but it meant the same thing: money—the one lubrication for love.

If the old lady wasn't dead, she was past caring. And it wouldn't take him but ninety seconds to have this wheel off . . .

He was starting to bend over to his task when the next sight froze him. The old lady had moved. He noticed it at first out of the corners of his eyes; then his head jerked up.

She was getting up. She had her two hands on the pavement and one knee up, and she was pushing to her feet. He could hear her laughing to herself. He felt the goose pimples breaking out down his back, and his scalp began to crawl like a battlefield of lice. If this kept up, his black kinky hair was going to turn out white as bleached cotton and straight as the beard of Jesus Christ.

He was watching the old lady, his brain trying to absorb the impact of what his eyes were registering, when the second car turned the corner. He didn't see it until it went past.

It was a big black sedan with the lights off, traveling at a hip-tightening clip, and it made a sound like someone blowing suddenly in his ear.

The old lady had got both feet planted and was standing bent over, bear-fashion, with all four feet and hands on the ground, just about to straighten up, when the big black sedan hit her in the rump.

He never knew how he saw it; the street was black dark, the old lady was dressed in black, the car was black. But he saw it. Either with his eyes or with his mind.

He saw the old lady flying through the air, arms and legs spread out, black garments spread out in the wind like a nuclear-powered vampire full of fresh virgin's blood. She was flying in an oblique line to the left; the black car was streaking straight ahead; and her snow-white hair was flying off to the right and rising, like a homing pigeon headed for the nest.

Furthermore, in the front seat of the black sedan were the dark silhouettes of three uniformed cops.

Now this joker had seen the face of violence in many make-ups. The quick, insensate leap across the river Styx was no news to him. He was not naive about the grisly jokes of death.

But what he saw now scrambled his brains. His head was running in all four directions; but his feet were just standing there like a yokel in a carnival harem. He turned around a couple of times as though he were looking for something. For what he didn't know.

Then he saw the car wheel leaning against the side of the jacked-up car. The wheel had a whitewall tire.

He grabbed the wheel and started running toward Convent Avenue. But the wheel was too heavy, so he put it down and began rolling it like a kid does a hoop.

That stretch of Convent Avenue goes down a steep hill toward 125th Street. When he came into Convent Avenue he turned the wheel down the hill. The wheel bounced over the curb and increased speed as it went down the hill. He kept up with it until it came to the next crossing. The wheel dropped from the curb and crossed the street. He stumbled slightly, and the wheel gained on him. When the wheel hit the next curb it bounced high in the air, and when it came down it went away like a supercharged sports car.

He looked down the hill and saw two cops standing beneath a streetlamp at the intersection of 126th or 127th Street. He put on the brakes and skidded to a stop, made a circle and went up the cross street he had passed. He disappeared into the night.

The wheel kept on down the street and knocked the legs out from underneath the two cops, knocked down a lady coming from the supermarket with a bag full of groceries, swerved out into the street, passed through the traffic of 125th Street without touching a thing, bounced over the sidewalk and crashed through the street-level door of a tenement facing the start of Convent Avenue.

A heavy-set, middle-aged man wearing a felt skull cap, old mended sweater, corduroy pants, and felt slippers, was emerging from the back apartment when the wheel crashed into the back wall of the hallway. He gave it a look, then did a double take. He looked about quickly, and, seeing no one, grabbed it, ducked back into his apartment and locked the door. It wasn't every day manna fell from heaven.

2

Roman Hill was driving the Cadillac. His thick, muscular shoulders, developed from handling a two-mule plow in the Alabama cotton fields, were hunched inside of his greasy leather jacket as though he were reining the four horsemen of the Apocalypse of St. John the Divine.

"Watch out!" Sassafras screamed. It was enough to raise the dead.

"Huh!" Air gushed from his mouth, and he gripped the wheel in his big, horny hands hard enough to break it.

He didn't see the old lady. It was the scream that did it. When he first saw the old lady she was caught in the left headlamp as though she had come out of the ground. His cocked gray eyes tried to leave his head in opposite directions.

"Look out!" he shouted as he tromped on the brake.

His two passengers sailed forward against the instrument panel, and he bumped his chest against the steer-rag wheel.

The old lady disappeared.

"My God, where she at?" he asked in a panic-stricken voice.

"You hit her!" Sassafras exclaimed.

"Step on it!" Mister Baron cried.

"Huh?" Roman's slack, tan face looked stupid from shock.

"Let's go, for God's sake," Mister Baron urged. "You've killed her. You don't want to stay here and get caught, do you?"

"Bleeding Jesus!" Roman muttered stupidly, and stepped on the gas.

The Cadillac took off as though it had been spurred in the cylinders.

"Stop!" Sassafras screamed again. "You ain't done nothing."

The Cadillac slowed.

"Don't listen to this woman, fool," Mister Baron shouted. "You'll get one to twenty years in jail."

"Why come?" Sassafras argued in a high keening voice. She had a long, oval face with under-developed features and coal-black skin; and her sloe eyes glittered like glass. "She walked right out in front of him; I'll swear to it."

"You're crazy, woman," Mister Baron hissed. "He hasn't got any driver's license; he hasn't got any insurance; he hasn't even got the car registered. They'd put him in jail just for driving it; and, for running over a woman and killing her, they'll lock him in Sing Sing and throw away the key."

"Of all the mother-raping luck," Roman said hoarsely as realization began penetrating his shock. "Here I is, ain't driven my new car a half hour, and done already ran over some woman and killed her stone-dead."

His forehead knotted in a tight frown and he sounded as though he might cry. But the Cadillac took off again with determination.

"Let's go back and see," Sassafras begged. "I didn't feel no bump."

"You wouldn't feel any bump in this car," Mister Baron said. "It could run over a railroad tie and you wouldn't feel it."

"He's right, honey," Roman agreed. "Ain't nothing but to hightail it now."

The big black Buick without lights cut in front of the Cadillac and a cop yelled out the open window: "Pull up!"

Roman had a notion to try to cut around the Buick and escape, but Mister Baron shrieked, "Stop—don't dent the fenders."

Sassafras gave him a scornful look.

All three cops piled out of the Buick and converged on the Cadillac with drawn pistols. One of the cops was white; he and one of the colored cops swung short-barreled .38 caliber police specials; the other had a long flat .38 Colt automatic.

"Get out with your hands up," one of the colored cops ordered in a hard, hurried voice.

"Right," the white cop echoed.

"What is this all about, officer?" Mister Baron said haughtily, assuming an indignant attitude.

"Manslaughter," the colored cop said harshly.

"Hit-and-run," the white cop echoed.

"We ain't hit nobody," Sassafras protested in her keening, nerve-scraping voice.

"Tell it to the judge," the colored cop said.

The white cop opened the outside door of the Cadillac and jerked Mister Baron from his seat. He handled him roughly, gripping the lapels of his chesterfield coat.

Roman had got out on the other side and was standing holding his hands level with his shoulders.

The white cop jerked Mister Baron out of the way so Sassafras could alight.

"Listen to me for a moment," Mister Baron said in a low, persuasive voice. "There hasn't anything happened that can't be settled between the few of us. The woman's not hurt bad. I could see in the rear-view mirror that she was getting up."

Mister Baron was small and effeminate with unusually expressive eyes for a man. They were a strange shade of light brown, fringed with long, black, curling lashes. But they fitted his girlish, heart-shaped face. His only masculine feature was the small fuzzy mustache and the bebop goatee that looked as though it might have been stuck on his chin with paste.

He was using his eyes now for all they were worth.

"If you want to be reasonable, this doesn't have to go to court.

And," he added, fluttering his lashes, "you can benefit in more ways than one—if you know what I mean."

The three cops exchanged glances.

Sassafras shook herself and looked at Mister Baron with infinite scorn. A small-boned, doll-like girl with a bottom like a duck's, she was wearing a gray imitation fur coat and a red knitted cap, which might have belonged to one of the seven dwarfs.

"If you're including me, you're barking up the wrong tree," she said.

"What's unusual about you, dear," Mister Baron said cattily.

"How much?" the white cop asked.

Mister Baron hesitated, appraising the cop. "Five hundred," he offered tentatively.

"Well, what about the old lady, if she ain't dead," Sassafras put in. "What you going to give her?"

"Let her lump it," Mister Baron said brutally.

"Put these two squares in the car," the white cop said.

One of the colored cops took Sassafras by the arm and steered her to the Buick.

Roman went docilely, still holding his hands shoulder-high. He looked like a joker who's bet his fortune on a sure thing and lost.

The cop hadn't troubled to search him. He didn't search him now. "Get in the back," he ordered.

Roman began to plead. "If you-all will give me just one more chance—"

The cop cut him off. "I ain't your mammy."

Roman got in and sat dejectedly, shoulders drooping, head so bowed his chin rested on his chest. Sassafras came in from the other side. She took one look at him and burst out crying.

The cops ignored them and turned toward Mister Baron, who stood confronting the white cop in the beam from the Cadillac's lamps.

"Douse those lights," the white cop said.

A colored cop walked over and turned off the lights.

The white cop cased the street. On the south side, old-fashioned residences with high stone steps, which had been converted into rooming houses or cut up into kitchenettes, were squeezed between apartment houses built for the overflowing white population in the 1920's, all taken over now by Ham's and Hagar's children.

On the north side was the high, crumbling stone wall of the convent, topped by the skeletons of trees. None of the convent buildings were visible from the street.

Aside from themselves, there was not a person in sight. Nothing moved but grit in the ice-cold wind.

"Five hundred all you got?" the white cop asked Mister Baron.

Mister Baron licked his lips, and his voice began to lilt. "You and me could talk business," he whispered.

"Come here," the white cop said.

Mister Baron walked up close to the white cop as though he were going to nestle in his arms.

The white cop turned him around and closed his windpipe with a half nelson while twisting his right arm behind his back. Mister Baron beat at him futilely with his left hand.

A colored cop closed in and drew a plaited leather sap. The other cop lifted Mister Baron's Homburg, and the first cop sapped him back of the ear. Mister Baron gave a low soft sigh and went liquid. The white cop lowered him to the street, and the colored cop put the Homburg over Mister Baron's face.

The white cop went through Mister Baron's pockets with rapid efficiency. He found two scented white silk handkerchiefs, a case of miscellaneous keys, a diamond engagement ring stuck tightly about a plastic tube of lipstick, an ivory comb containing strands of Mister Baron's long wavy hair, a black rubber object shaped like a banana attached to an elastic band, and a package of one-hundred-dollar bills wrapped in greasy brown paper.

He grunted. The colored cops watched him with silent concentration. He put the package of bills into his side coat pocket and stuffed the remaining items back into Mister Baron's side overcoat pocket.

"Leave him here?" a colored cop asked.

"Naw, let's put him in the car," the white cop said.

"We'd better get going," the other cop urged. "We're wasting too much time."

"No need to hurry now," the white cop said. "We got it made."

Without replying, the two colored cops picked up Mister Baron and carried him toward the Buick, while the white cop held the back door open.

Neither Roman nor Sassafras had seen a thing.

"What's happened to him?" Sassafras stopped crying long enough to ask.

"He fainted," the white cop said. "Get over."

She moved toward the middle, and they propped Mister Baron in the corner of the seat.

"Hey, boy," the white cop called to Roman.

Roman looked around.

"I'm going to impound your car, and my partners are going to stay here until the ambulance comes and then bring you to the station. And I don't want any trouble out of you folks; you understand?"

"Yassuh," Roman said duly, as though the world had come to an end.

"All right," the white cop said. "Just let this be a lesson; you can't buy justice."

"It weren't him," Sassafras said.

"You just keep him quiet if you know what's good for you," the cop said, and slammed the door.

He walked unhurriedly back to the Cadillac. One of the colored cops was sitting behind the wheel, the other sitting beside him. The white cop sat on the outside and slammed the door.

The cop driving started the motor and began easing off without turning on the lights. The big golden Cadillac crept silently around the back end of the Buick and had started past before Sassafras noticed it.

"Look, they is taking our car," she cried.

Roman was too dejected to look up. "He's impounding it," he muttered.

"It ain't just him; it's all of them," she said.

Roman's cocked eyes came up in a startled face. "Why you reckon they is doing that?" he asked stupidly.

"I bet my life they is stealing it," she said.

Roman jumped as though a time bomb had gone off in his pants. "Stealing my car!" he shouted, his hard, cable-like muscles coming into violent life.

He had the door open and was out on the pavement and pursuing the golden Cadillac before she could start screaming. She opened her mouth and let loose a scream that caused windows to pop open all up and down the street.

Roman was the only one who didn't hear her. His big, muscle-bound body was rolling as he ran, as though the sloping black pavement were the deck of a ship caught in a storm at sea. He was tugging at something stuck down his pants leg, beneath his leather jacket. Finally he came out with a big, rusty .45 caliber revolver, but before he had a chance to fire it the Cadillac had turned the corner and disappeared from sight.

A joker on a motorcycle with a sidecar was pulling out from the curb when the big Cadillac suddenly bore down on him and the driver switched on the lights. He did a quick turn back toward the curb. From the corners of his eyes he saw a golden Cadillac pass at a blinding speed. The silhouettes of three cops occupying the front seat lashed briefly across his vision. His brain did a double take and flipped.

This joker had seen this Cadillac a short time before. At that time the occupants had been two civilians and a woman. There couldn't be but one Cadillac like that in Harlem, he was sure. If there was such a Cadillac. If he wasn't just blowing his top.

This joker was wearing dark-brown coveralls, a woolen-lined army fatigue jacket, and a fur-lined, dark-plaid hunter's cap. There wasn't but one joker looking like this outside on this bitter cold night.

"No, it ain't true," the joker said to himself. "Either I ain't me or what I seen ain't that."

While he was trying to figure out which was which a big black sedan screamed around the corner with its bright lights splitting open the black-dark night.

It was a Buick sedan, and it looked familiar. But not nearly so familiar as the woman he'd seen a short time before in the golden Cadillac. However, now the freak with the coonskin cap who had been driving the Cadillac was driving the Buick.

All of it was so crazy it was reassuring. He bent over the handlebars of his motorcycle and began laughing as though he had gone crazy himself.

"Haw haw haw." He laughed, and then began talking to himself. "Whatever it is I is dreaming, one thing is for sure—ain't none of it true."

3

The switchboard in the precinct station was jammed.

The switchboard sergeant relayed the reports to Desk Lieutenant Anderson in a bored, monotonous voice: "There's a woman who lives across the street from the convent says murder and rape taking place in the street . . ."

Lieutenant Anderson yawned. "Every time a man beats his wife some busybody calls in and says she's being raped and murdered—the wife, I mean. And God knows some of them could use a little of it—the busybodies, I mean."

". . . another woman from the same vicinity. Says someone is torturing a dog . . ."

"Tell her we're sending an officer over right away," Anderson said. "Tell her dogs are our best friends."

"She hung up. But here's another one. Claims the nuns are having an orgy."

"Something's going on," Anderson conceded. "Send Joe Abrams and his partner over to take a look."

The sergeant switched on the radio. "Come in, Joe Abrams."

Joe Abrams came in.

"Take a look along the south side of the convent."

"Right," Joe Abrams said.

"Patrolman Stick calling from a box on 125th Street," the sergeant said to Anderson. "Claims he and his partner, Sam Price, were attacked and unfooted by a flying saucer someone has released in the neighborhood."

"Order them to report here before going off duty for an alcohol test," Anderson said sternly.

The sergeant chuckled as he relayed the order. Then he plugged in another call, and his face went grim.

"Man giving his name as Benjamin Zazuly, calling from the Paris Bar on 125th Street, reporting a double murder. Says two men dead on the sidewalk in front of the bar. One a white man. A third man unconscious. Thinks he's Casper Holmes . . ."

Anderson's fist came down on the desk, and his lean, hard face went bitter. "Goddammit, everything happens to me," he said, but the moment he had said it he regretted it.

"Get the other two cars over there," he directed in a steady voice. The veins throbbed in his temples, and his pale-blue eyes looked remote.

He waited until the sergeant had contacted the two prowl cars and dispatched them to the scene. Then he said, "Get Jones and Johnson."

While the sergeant was calling for Jones and Johnson to come in, Anderson said anxiously, "Let us hope nothing has happened to Holmes."

The sergeant couldn't get Jones and Johnson.

Anderson stood up. "Keep trying," he ordered. "I'm going to run over and take a quick look for myself."

The reason the sergeant couldn't get Grave Digger Jones and Coffin Ed Johnson is that they were in the back room of Mammy Louise's pork store eating hot "chicken feetsy," a Geechy dish of stewed chicken feet, rice, okra, and red chili peppers. On a cold night like this it kept a warm fire burning in the stomach, and the white, tender gristle of the chicken feet gave a solid packing to the guts.

There were three wooden tables covered with oilcloth of such a bilious color that only the adhesive consistency of Mammy Louise's

Geechy stews could hold the food in the stomach. Against the side wall was a coal-burning stove flanked by copper water tasks. Pots of cooking foods bubbled on the hot lids, giving the small, close room the steamy, luxurious feeing of a Turkish bath.

Grave Digger and Coffin Ed were sitting at the table farthest from the stove, their coats draped over the backs of wooden chairs. Their beat-up black hats hung above their overcoats on nails in the outside wall. Sweat beaded on their skulls underneath their short-cropped, kinky hair and streamed down their dark, intent faces. Coffin Ed's hair was peppered with gray. He had a crescent-shaped scar on the right-side top of his skull, where Grave Digger had hit him with his pistol barrel, the time he had gone berserk after being blinded by acid thrown into his face. That had been more than three years ago, and the acid scars had been covered by skin, grafted from his thigh. But the new skin was a shade or so lighter than his natural face skin and it had been grafted on in pieces. The result was that Coffin Ed's face looked as though it had been made up in Hollywood for the role of the Frankenstein monster. Grave Digger's rough, lumpy face could have belonged to any number of hard, Harlem characters.

Grave Digger sucked the gristle from his last chicken foot and spat the small white bones onto the pile on his plate.

"I'll bet you a bottle he don't make it," he said in a low voice, barely audible.

Coffin Ed looked at his wrist watch. "What kind of bet is that," he replied in a similar tone of voice. "It's already five minutes to twelve, and she got off at eleven-thirty. You think she's waiting for him."

"Naw, but he thinks so."

They glanced surreptitiously at a man sitting in a worn wooden armchair in the corner beside the stove. He was a short, fat, bald-headed man with the round, black, mobile face of a natural-born comedian. Except for an overcoat, he was dressed for the street. He was staring across at them with a pleading look.

He was Mister Louise, Mammy's husband. He had been picking

up a hot little brownskin waitress at the Fischer Cafeteria next to the 125th Street railroad station every Saturday night since the new year began.

But Mammy Louise had got a bulldog. It was a six-year-old bulldog of a dirty white color with a mouth big enough to let in full-grown cats. It sat on its haunches directly in front of Mister Louise's shinily shod feet and stared up into his desperate face with a lidded, unblinking look. Its pink mouth was wide open as it panted in the steamy heat; its red tongue hung down its chest. There was a big wet spot on the floor where it had been drooling as though it would like nothing better than a hunk of Mister Louise's fat black meat.

"He wants us to help him," Coffin Ed whispered.

"And get ourselves chawed up by that dog instead of him."

Mammy Louise looked up from the stove where she had been stirring a pot. She was fatter than Mister Louise, but not quite as tall. She wore an old woolen bathrobe over an old jersey dress, under which were layers of warm woolen underclothing. Over the bathrobe she wore a black knitted shawl; her head was protected by a man's beaver hat with a turned-up brim, and her feet were encased in fur-lined woodsmen's boots.

She was a Geechy, born and raised in the swamps south of Tater Patch, South Carolina. Geechies are a mélange of runaway African slaves and Seminole Indians, native to the Carolinas and Florida. Their mother tongue is a mixture of African dialects and the Seminole language; and she spoke English with a strange, indefinable accent that sounded somewhat similar to a conference of crows.

"What you two p'licemens whispering about so seriously?" she asked suspiciously.

It took a moment before they could piece together what she said.

"We got a bet," Grave Digger replied with a straight face.

"Naw we haven't," Coffin Ed denied.

"You p'licemens," she said scornfully. "Gamblin' an' carryin' on an' whippin' innocent folkses' heads with your big pistols."

"Not if they're innocent," Grave Digger contradicted.

"Don't tell me," she said argumentatively. "I has seen you." She curled her thick, sensuous lips. "Whippin' grown men about as if they was children. Mister Louise wouldn't stand for it," she added, looking slyly from her husband's desperate face to the slobbering bulldog. "Get up, Mister Louise, and show these p'licemens how you captured them train robbers that time."

Mister Louise looked at her gratefully and started to his feet. The bulldog raised up and growled a warning; Mister Louise slumped back into his seat.

Mammy Louise winked her off eye at the detectives. "Mister Louise ain't so pokey tonight," she explained. "He just want to set here and keep me company."

"So we noticed," Coffin Ed said.

Mister Louise stared longingly at the long-barreled, nickel-plated .38 caliber revolvers sticking from the two detectives' shoulder holsters.

They heard the front door to the store open and bang shut. Feet stamped. A whisky-thick voice called, "Hey, Mammy Louise, come out here and give me a pot of them frozen chitterlings."

She waddled through the curtained doorway leading to the store. They heard her opening a five-gallon milk can and shuffling about, and the customer protesting, "I don't wants them loose chitterlings; I wants some frozen chitterlings," and her sharp reply, "If you wants to eat 'em frozen just take 'em outside and freeze 'em; hit's cold enough."

Grave Digger said, "Mammy Louise can't stand this Northern climate."

"She got enough fat to keep her warm at the North Pole," Coffin Ed replied.

"The trouble is, her fat gets cold."

Mister Louise begged in a piteous voice, "One of you gentlemens shoot him for me, won't you." He glanced toward the curtained doorway and added, "I'll pay you."

"It wouldn't kill him," Coffin Ed replied solemnly.

"Bullets would just bounce off his head," Grave Digger supplemented.

Mammy Louise came back and looked at her husband suspiciously. Then she said to the detectives, "Your car is talking."

"I'll get it," Grave Digger said, getting to his feet before he'd finished saying it.

He slipped an arm through his jacket, grabbed his hat from the peg and pushed through the curtains as he poked his second arm into its sleeve.

The bulldog rolled its pink eyes at his receding figure and looked at Mammy Louise for instructions. But she paid it no attention. She was half moaning to herself. "Trouble, always trouble in dis wicked city. Whar Ah comes from—"

"There ain't no law," Coffin Ed cut her off as he put on his jacket. "Folks cut one another's throats and go on about their business."

"It's better than getting kilt by the law," she argued. "You can't pay for one death by another one. Salvation ain't the swapping market."

Coffin Ed jammed his hat on his head, turned up the brim and slipped into his overcoat.

"Tell it to the voters, Mammy," he said absently as he took down Grave Digger's overcoat and straightened out a sleeve. "I didn't make these laws."

"I'll tell it to everybody," she said.

Grave Digger came back in a hurry. His face was set.

"Hell's broke loose on the street," he said, poking his arm into the coat Coffin Ed held for him.

"We'd better hop it, then," Coffin Ed said.

Unnoticed by anyone but Mister Louise, the bulldog had moved over to block the curtained doorway. When Grave Digger moved toward it, the dog planted its feet and growled.

Grave Digger's long, gleaming, nickel-plated revolver came out in his hand like a feat of legerdemain, but Mammy Louise swooped down on the dog and dragged it off before he did it injury.

"Not dem, Lawd Jim, mah God, dawg," she cried. "You can't stop dem from goin' nowhere. Them is de *mens.*"

4

The small, battered black sedan parked at the curb in front of Mammy Louise's *Hog Store: open day & night* was still talking when they came out on the street. Grave Digger slid beneath the wheel, and Coffin Ed went around and climbed in from the other side.

The store was on 124th Street between Seventh and Eighth Avenues, and the car was pointing toward Seventh.

The Paris Bar was due north as the bird flies on 125th Street, midway between the Apollo Bar and the Palm Café and across the street from Blumstein's Department Store.

It was ten minutes by foot, if you were on your way to church, about two and a half minutes if your old lady was chasing you with a razor.

Coffin Ed checked his watch when Grave Digger mashed the starter. The little car might have looked like a bow-legged turtle, but it ran like an antelope.

It passed the Theresa Hotel, going up the wrong side of the street, bright lights on and siren screaming. Jokers in the lobby staring out the windows scattered like a hurricane had passed. They made it in thirty-three seconds.

Two prowl cars and Lieutenant Anderson's black sedan were parked in front of the Paris Bar, taking up all the available space. Save for the cops standing about in clusters, the street was deserted.

"One's a white man," Grave Digger said.

"What else?" Coffin Ed replied.

What he meant was what else could keep the black citizens away from the circus provided by a killing.

"Butts going to jump," Grave Digger added as he made a sharp-angled turn and squeezed between the front car and a fireplug, jumping the curb.

Before he had dragged to a stop, crosswise the sidewalk, just short of banging into the grilled front of a drugstore adjacent to the Paris Bar, they saw the three prone figures on the sidewalk.

The one nearest wore a belted trench coat and a dark snapbrim hat that was still clinging to his head. He lay that on his belly, his legs spread and his feet resting on his toes. His left arm was folded down beside him with the palm turned up; his right arm was flung out at an angle, still gripping a short-barreled revolver. Street light shone on the soles of his shoes, showing runover rubber heels and recent toecaps. The top part of his face was shaded by his hat brim, but orange light from the neon bar sign lit the lower part, showing the tip of a hooked nose and a long, pointed chin and leaving the thin, compressed lips invisible, so that the face seemed to lack a mouth.

One glance was enough to tell that he was dead.

The Paris Bar had a stainless-steel front framing the two big plate-glass windows that tanked the doorway. The left-side steel baseboard directly behind the stiff was punctured with bullet holes.

With the second stiff, it was different. He lay piled up like a wet towel directly in front of the door. His smooth, handsome black face peered from folds of gay-colored clothes with a look of infinite surprise. He didn't look so much dead from gunshot as from shock; but the small, round, purple-lipped hole above his right temple told the story.

The third figure was encircled by cops.

Grave Digger and Coffin Ed alighted and converged on the first stiff.

"Two hits through the top of the hat," Grave Digger observed, his gaze roving. "He was lying on his belly and they nailed the hat on tighter."

"Two in the right shoulder and one in the left neck," said Coffin Ed. "Somebody sure wanted this son dead."

"No one man scored five hits on this guy and him with a gun in his hand," Grave Digger stated.

"The way I see it, two or more guns were shooting from down there where Casper is lying, and a third gun cross-fired from a car parked at the curb."

"Yeah," Grave Digger agreed, counting the bullet holes in the stainless-steel baseboard. "Somebody was using an automatic in the car and missed all ten times."

"This guy was lying flat, and the gun in the car was shooting over him, but it gave the ones in front a chance to ice him."

Grave Digger nodded. "This guy knew his business, but he was outgunned."

"Over here!" Lieutenant Anderson called.

He and a white precinct detective named Haggerty and two prowl-car cops were standing about an unconscious colored man stretched out on the sidewalk.

Grave Digger and Coffin Ed glanced briefly at the second stiff as they ambled past.

"Know him?" Grave Digger asked.

"One of the girl-boys," Coffin Ed said.

Detective Haggerty skinned back his teeth when they approached. "Every time I see you big fellows I think of two hog farmers lost in the city," he greeted.

Grave Digger flipped him a look. "The office wit."

Coffin Ed ignored him.

Both of them stared down at the unconscious figure. He had

been turned over onto his back, and his bowler placed beneath his head for a pillow. His hands were folded across his chest, and his eyes were closed. But for the labored breathing, he might have been dead.

He was wearing a navy-blue cashmere coat with hand-stitched lapels and patch pockets. His shirt was hidden by a black silk scarf looped at the throat. The trousers were of a dark-blue flannel with a soft chalk stripe. Black calfskin shoes, practically new, finished the ensemble.

He had a broad, smooth-shaven face with a square, aggressive-looking chin. The black skin had a creamy, massaged look, and the short, carefully clipped kinky hair was snow-white. His appearance was impressive.

"Casper looks natural," Coffin Ed said with a straight face.

"He was sapped behind the left ear," Lieutenant Anderson stated.

"How do you figure it?" Grave Digger asked.

"It seems as though Holmes was robbed, but the rest doesn't figure," Anderson confessed.

"Laughing-boy yonder must have stepped out the bar to watch the bullets passing," Haggerty cracked, amused by his own humor.

"One he didn't see," a white cop added, grinning.

Anderson wiped off the grin with a look.

"Who's the gunman?" Coffin Ed asked.

"We haven't made him," Anderson said. "Haven't touched him. We're waiting for the M. E. and the crew from Homicide."

"What do the witnesses say?"

"Witnesses?"

"Somebody in the bar must have seen the whole caper."

"Yeah, but we haven't got any of them to admit it," Anderson said. "You know how it is when a white man gets killed. No one wants to get involved. I've sent for the wagon, and I'm going to take them all in."

"Let me talk to them first," Coffin Ed said.

"Okay, give it a try."

Coffin Ed ambled toward the entrance to the bar, which was being guarded by a white patrolman.

Grave Digger looked enquiringly at a white civilian who had edged into the group.

"This is Mr. Zazuly," Anderson said. "He got here right after the shooting and telephoned the station."

"What did he see?" Grave Digger asked.

"When I got here the street was overrun with people," Mr. Zazuly said, his magnified eyes blinking rapidly behind the thick lenses of his horn-rimmed spectacles. "The two men were lying there just as you see them, and not an officer in sight."

"He's an accountant for Blumstein's," Anderson explained.

"Did he hear the shooting?"

"Of course I heard the shooting. It sounded like the Second World War. And not a policeman in sight." His round, owlish face glared from a mohair muffler with a look of extreme outrage. "Gang wars on a main thoroughfare like this. Right out in the broad open," he went on indignantly. "Where were the police, I ask you?"

Grave Digger looked sheepish.

No one answered him.

"I'm going to write a complaint to the Commissioner," he threatened.

The sound of a siren grew quickly in the night.

"Here comes the ambulance," Anderson said with relief.

The red eye of the ambulance was coming up 125th Street fast, from the direction of Lenox Avenue.

Grave Digger addressed Mr. Zazuly directly. "And that's all you saw?"

"What did you expect him to see?" Haggerty cracked. "Look at those specs."

The ambulance double-parked beside a prowl car, and the cops stood by silently while the intern made a cursory examination.

"Can you give him something to bring him to?" Anderson asked him.

"Give him what?" the intern replied.

"Well, when will he be able to talk?"

"Can't say, Inspector, he might have a concussion."

"I see you're going to get ahead fast," Anderson commented.

Nothing more was said while Casper Holmes was rolled onto the stretcher and moved.

Anderson glanced at his watch. "Homicide ought to be getting here," he said anxiously.

"The stiffs won't spoil in this weather," Haggerty said, turning up the collar of his overcoat and putting his back to the ice-cold, dust-laden wind.

"I'm going to see how Ed's making out," Grave Digger said, and strolled toward the entrance to the Paris.

When Coffin Ed entered the Paris Bar, not one person looked in his direction.

It was a long, narrow room, with the bar running the length of the left side, taking up all the space. Customers sat on bar stools or stood; there were no tables.

The usual Saturday night crowd was gathered, bitchy young men wearing peacock clothes with bright-colored caps, blue and silver and gold and purple, perched atop greasy curls straight from the barbershops at seven dollars a treatment. And the big, strong, rough-looking men who made life wonderful for them. But there was not a woman present.

Coffin Ed was not a moralist. But their cliquish quality of freezing up on an outsider grated on his nerves.

"Don't everybody talk at once," he shouted from the doorway.

No one said a word.

To a man, they were staring into their drinks as though competing in a contest of three wise monkeys: See nothing; hear nothing; say nothing. The contest was progressing toward a dead heat.

The three bartenders were rinsing glasses with an industriousness that would have gotten them all blacklisted by the bartenders' union.

Coffin Ed began swelling at the gills. His gaze flickered dangerously down the line, seeking a likely candidate to begin with. But they were all equally engrossed in silence.

"Don't try to give me that silent treatment," he warned. "We're all colored folks together."

Someone in back giggled softly.

The uniformed white cop guarding the rear door stared at him with a dead-pan expression.

Coffin Ed's temper flared, and the grafted patches on his face began to twitch.

He spoke to the back of the joker on the first stool. "All right, buddy boy, let's start with you. Which way did they go?"

The girlish young man continued to stare into his drink as though he were stone-deaf. The indirect lighting from the bar gave his smooth brown face a bemused look. His luminescent silver cap gleamed faintly like swamp-fire.

He was drinking a tall frappé highball of dark rum with a streak of grenadine running down the center, called a "Josephine Baker." If La Baker herself had been reclining stark nude in the bottom of his glass, he could not have given her any more attention.

Coffin Ed took him roughly by the shoulder and tamed him about. "Which way did they go?" he repeated in a rasping voice.

The young man looked at him from big, brown, bedroom eyes that seemed incapable of comprehending anything but love.

"Go, sir? Who go?" he lisped.

Face jumping in a sudden flash of rage, Coffin Ed slapped him left-handed from the bar stool. The young man crashed against the wall and crumpled in a lump.

Eyes pivoted in his direction and pivoted away. He wasn't hurt so much as stunned. He thought it best just to lie there.

Coffin Ed looked at the next joker in line. He was an older man, dressed conservatively. Answers gushed from his mouth without his being questioned. "They went west, that is, down 125th Street, I don't mean to California."

Coffin Ed's face looked so macabre the man had to swallow before he could continue.

"They was in a black Buick. There was three of 'em. One was driving and the other two pulled off the heist."

He ran out of breath.

"Did you get the license?"

"License!" He looked as though Coffin Ed had abused his mother. "What would I be doing getting their license? They looked like straight cops when they drove up, and for all I know they might just as well be straight cops."

"Cops!" Coffin Ed stiffened.

"And when they took off I was lying on the floor like everybody else."

"You said they were cops!"

"I don't mean they actually was cops," the joker amended hastily. "I figure you would know if they was real sure enough cops. All I means is they looked like cops."

"In uniform?" Coffin Ed was taut as a crane cable, and his voice came in a rasping whisper.

"How else would I know if they looked like cops. I don't mean you, suh," the joker hastened to add with an ingratiating smile. "Everybody around here knows you is the *man*, no matter what you wears. All I means is these cops was dressed in cops' uniforms. Of course I ain't had no way of knowing whether they was cops or not. Naturally I wasn't going to ask to see their shields. All I know is what I seen, and they—"

Coffin Ed was thinking fast. He cut the joker off. "Colored men?"

"Two of 'em was. One was a white man."

Heistmen impersonating cops. He was trying to remember when was the last time that was worked in Harlem. Generally that was a big-time deal.

"What did he look like?"

"Look like? Who look like?"

He had been concentrating so hard on trying to put the puzzle together that he had forgotten the joker. His gaze came back in hard focus.

"The white man. Don't start getting cute."

"It was just like I say, boss, he looked like a cop. You know how it is, boss," he added slyly, giving Coffin Ed a confidential wink. "All these white cops look just alike."

Under ordinary circumstances Coffin Ed would have passed that one by; the color angle worked just about the same on the force as it did in private life. He had played the "all us is black folks together" line himself on entering. But he wasn't in the mood for comic patter.

"Listen, punk, this ain't funny, this is murder," he said.

"Don't look at me, boss, I ain't done it," the joker said, throwing up his hands in comic pantomime as though to ward off a blow.

He didn't really expect a blow, but he got one. Coffin Ed's fists parted his hands and popped him in the left eye, and he sailed off the stool to join the other joker on the floor.

The customers began to mutter. He was getting their full attention now, and they were squirming into life.

The next joker in line was standing up. He was a big, rough-looking black man in a leather jacket and a cowskin fez. But suddenly he felt too big for the situation and was trying unsuccessfully to make himself smaller.

Coffin Ed measured him with bloodshot eyes. "Do you belong to the league, too?" he asked through gritted teeth.

"League? Nawsuh, boss. I mean if it's the wrong league I sure don't belong to it."

"The know-nothing league."

"Not me, boss." The big joker showed Coffin Ed a mouthful of teeth as proof that he didn't belong to any league, unless it was the dentist's league. "I ain't scairt to tell the truth. I'll tell you everything I seen, I swear 'fore God. 'Course, that ain't much, but—"

"You saw two men get shot to death."

"Heard it, boss. I wasn't in no position to see."

"Three men masqueraded as cops—"

"I ain't seen but two, boss."

"Robbed a man in broad view right outside of this joint—"

"I couldn't swear to it, boss; I didn't seen that."

"What did they get?"

"*Get?*" The joker acted as though he were unfamiliar with the word.

"Take?"

"Take? If they took anything, boss, I ain't seen it. I thought they was just a mess of cops doing their dirty work."

Coffin Ed flipped.

He looped a right hook to the big joker's solar plexus, saw his mouth balloon with air. The cowskin fez flew from the big joker's head as he jackknifed forward. Coffin Ed caught him back of the neck with a loose, pulling grip, jerked his head down and uppercut him in the face with his right knee. It was a good gimmick; the knee was supposed to smash the joker's nose and fill his head with shooting stars. It worked nine times out of ten. But the big joker had his mouth open from the solar plexus punch, and his teeth crashed into Coffin Ed's kneecap like the jaws of a bear trap.

Coffin Ed grunted with pain as his leg went stiff, and clutched the back of the big joker's leather jacket to keep from going down. The big joker butted him in the belly in a blind panic, trying to escape. Coffin Ed went down on his back, clinging to the leather jacket; and the big joker plunged forward over him, headed for the door. Coffin Ed pulled at the leather jacket in a choking rage. The jacket turned wrong side out, imprisoning the joker's arm and halting the forward plunge of his shoulders. But the rest of him kept on going, and he turned in a somersault and landed on his back. Coffin Ed reared up on his shoulders, made a half spin and kicked the big joker on the side of the jaw from topside down. The big joker shuddered and passed out.

Coffin Ed clutched the rim of the bar and pulled to his feet, favoring his game leg. He looked about for the next man in line. But there wasn't any line.

The customers had crowded to the back of the room and were beginning to panic. Knives lashed, and they were pushing and threatening one another.

The white cop at the back door was shouting, "Get back! Get away from me or I'll shoot!"

Slowly and deliberately, Coffin Ed drew the long-barreled, nickel-plated .38 revolver from its shoulder holster.

"Now I want some straight answers from you minstrel-show comedians," he said in a voice that grated on the nerves.

Someone let out a womanish scream.

Grave Digger came in from the street. Without taking a second look he opened his big mouth and shouted at the top of his voice: "Straighten up!" Before his big voice bounced from the walls he had his big nickel-plated revolver, the twin of Coffin Ed's, out in his hand, in plain sight of everyone arrested by his voice.

Coffin Ed relaxed. A grim smile played about the edges of his scarred lips.

"Count off!" he bellowed in a voice to match Grave Digger's.

For good measure they fired four shots into the newly decorated ceiling.

Everybody froze. Not a whisper was heard. No one dared breathe.

Coffin Ed had killed a man for breaking wind. Grave Digger had shot both eyes out of a man who was holding a loaded automatic. The story was in Harlem that these two black detectives would kill a dead man in his coffin if he so much as moved.

The next moment cops of all descriptions erupted from the street. The Homicide crew had arrived and they invaded in force; a lieutenant and two detectives with their pistols out, a third detective with a submachine gun. The precinct lieutenant, Anderson, followed, with Haggerty at his heels and two uniformed cops bringing up the rear.

"What's this? What's happening? What gives?" the Homicide lieutenant shouted harshly.

"Just them two cowboys from the Harlem Q. ranch rounding up a passel of rustlers," Haggerty cracked.

"Jesus Christ," Anderson said, as though gasping. "Use a little discretion, men. With what's already happened you'll have us filling our pants."

"We're just trying to get some sense out of these people," Grave Digger said.

The lieutenant from Homicide stared at him in popeyed amazement. "You—you mean all you're trying to do is make these witnesses talk?"

"It works," Grave Digger said.

"It quiets them," Coffin Ed added. "You'll notice it has a soothing effect on their nerves."

All eyes turned toward the quiet, passive people crowded toward the rear.

"Well, I'll be God-damned," the Homicide lieutenant said. "Now I've seen everything."

"Naw you ain't," Haggerty said. "You ain't seen nothing yet."

"The wagon's here. We're going to take these people to the station for questioning," Anderson said.

"Give us fifteen minutes with them first," Grave Digger requested.

In the brief silence that followed, the head bartender said, "Don't let 'em close us up, chief—I'll tell you all about it."

Eyes swung in his direction. He was a well-fed, intelligent-looking man of about thirty-five, who could have been palmed off as a Baptist preacher from one of the poorer congregations.

"See what I mean?" Haggerty said.

"Come on," Anderson said. "Your wit needs oiling."

5

"It began with Snake Hips," the bartender said, polishing a glass to occupy his hands.

"Snake Hips," Grave Digger said incredulously. "He's the female impersonator at the Down Beat Club up the street."

"The *danseur*," the bartender corrected with a straight face.

"What did he have to do with it?" Coffin Ed asked.

"Nothing. He was just dancing. He danced outside and we were watching him, and that's how we saw it happen."

"Without a coat or hat? By himself? He left here and went outside to dance in this weather without a hat or coat—by himself?" Disbelief was written all over Grave Digger's face.

"He was just bitching off," the bartender explained. He held the glass up to the light, blew on it and began polishing again. "He had got himself a new lover, and he was just low-rating the man who used to be his lover before. You know how these people are; when they get mad at you, they get out in the street and start scandalizing you."

"Who is the man?" Coffin Ed asked.

"Sir?"

"The man who was his former lover."

The bartender looked for a place to hang his gaze. Finally he settled on the glass he was polishing. If his skin had been lighter, the blush would have showed. Finally he whispered, "It was me, sir."

Grave Digger brushed it off. "All right, let's finish with Snake Hips. Who is his current lover?"

"I'm not sure, sir—you know how these things are with these people—" He choked a little, but they let it pass. "I mean, one never really knows. He's been going around with a person called Black Beauty."

They didn't ask him if this person was a man, and he didn't elaborate.

"But Black Beauty's been seen around town with a man named Baron; and I know for a fact Baron's been hanging around with a white man—I don't know his name."

"You ever see him—the white man?" Coffin Ed asked.

"Yes, sir."

They avoided asking him where.

"Was he one of the trio—the heistmen?" Grave Digger asked.

"Oh no, sir. He wasn't anything like that. He was a sort of a gentleman type—you find on Broadway," he amended.

"All right, that does for Snake Hips," Grave Digger said as they stored away the information against future use. "You know Casper Holmes by sight?"

"Yes, sir, he's a customer here."

"What?"

The bartender shrugged slightly, spreading his hands, holding the glass in one and the towel in the other.

"Sometimes. Not a regular. It's just near his office, which is upstairs, and he drops by sometimes for a short one."

"Did he pass by the front here?" Coffin Ed asked.

"Yes, sir. He must have just come from his office. But he didn't stop in here. Snake Hips was dancing, and he passed right by him as if he didn't see him—like he had something on his mind."

"Does he know Snake Hips?"

The bartender lowered his eyes. "It's possible, sir. Mr. Holmes gets around."

"Could Snake Hips' dancing act have been a tip-off?"

"Oh, I'm sure it wasn't that. He was just trying to drag me. You see I got a wife and two children—"

"And you still got time for these boys?"

"Well, that was it. I didn't—"

"Let him go on," Grave Digger said harshly. "So Casper didn't see him, or rather didn't acknowledge him."

"It was more that. He must have seen him. But he was walking in a hurry, looking straight ahead and carrying a pigskin bag—"

Both detectives stiffened to alert.

"Brief case?" Grave Digger asked in an urgent whisper.

"Why, yes, sir. A pigskin brief case with a handle. It looked new. He was going toward Seventh Avenue, and I figured he was going to take a taxi."

"Let us do the guessing."

"Well, he usually parks his car out front. It wasn't there, so I figured—" Grave Digger's look cut him off. "Well, anyway, he was just past the doorway when a black Buick sedan pulled to the curb—"

"There was parking space?"

"Yes, sir—it so happened that two cars had just pulled off."

"You know whose they were?"

"The cars? No, sir. I think the drivers came from—or rather the passengers, there was a party of 'em—came from the Palm Café."

"Casper notice it?"

"He didn't act like it. He kept on walking. Then two cops—or rather men dressed in cops' uniforms—got out and another one stayed behind the wheel. My first thought was that Mr. Holmes was carrying valuables and the cops were a bodyguard. But Mr. Holmes tried to walk past them—between them rather, because they sort of separated when he tried to pass them—"

"Where was the white man?"

"He was on Mr. Holmes' right, toward the street. Mr. Holmes was carrying the brief case on that side. Then they took him by the arms; one took hold of each arm. Mr. Holmes seemed surprised, then mad."

"You couldn't see his face from here."

"No, sir. But his back stiffened, and he looked like he was mad, and I know he was saying something because I could see the side of his face working. It was lit by the sign light, and it seemed as if he was shouting, but of course I couldn't hear him."

"Well, go on," Grave Digger urged. "We haven't got all night."

"Well, sir, that was the first I figured there was something wrong. Then the next thing I knew I saw the white man knock Mr. Holmes' hat off; he sort of flicked it off from behind so that it fell in front of Mr. Holmes. And at the same time the colored cop—man—sapped Mr. Holmes behind the left ear; he was on Mr. Holmes' left side."

"Did you see the sap?"

"Not too well. It looked like an ordinary leather-bound sap with a whalebone handle to me."

"Did he hit him again?"

"No sir, once was enough. Mr. Holmes went down like he was sitting, and the white man took the pigskin bag out of his hand."

"Who else in the bar here saw this happen?"

"I don't think anybody else saw it. You see, the customers face this way and only us bartenders face in that direction, and the other bartenders was busy. It wasn't like they had made any noise. I saw it, but I couldn't hear a sound."

"What about Snake Hips? Didn't he see what was happening, or was he too far gone."

"He hadn't been banging, if that's what you mean. But he was dancing in a slow circle, doing a sort of shake dance, and he had his back to them."

"But they must have seen him."

"Must have. But they didn't pay him no attention. As far as they were concerned, he was harmless as a lamppost."

"Why didn't you telephone the police?" Grave Digger asked.

"I didn't have time. I was going to, but the next thing I knew I heard a shot. A man appeared right outside of this window like he had come from nowhere. When I first heard the shot my first thought was they'd shot Snake Hips—the silly fool—then I saw this man standing there with one of those short bulldog-looking pistols held straight out in his right hand. Then I heard him say in a hard, dry voice, 'Get 'em up!' "

"You heard him?"

"Yes, sir. You see, he didn't speak until after he had shot; and at the sound of the shot everybody inside of here went stone-quiet."

"That's when the two heistmen started shooting," Coffin Ed surmised.

"No, sir. I don't know what they did because I wasn't looking at them no more. But they didn't start shooting with that man pointing that gun at them. But the cop—man—in the car started shooting. It was dark inside the car, and I could see the orange lashes."

He ceased polishing the glass for the moment, and his brown face went ashy at the memory.

"Of course the man wasn't shooting at me, but the gun was pointing this way, and it seemed like I was looking down the barrel. I was scared enough to drop six babies, because it looked like he never was going to stop shooting." He wiped sweat drops from his ashy face with the polishing towel.

"Eleven-shot automatic," Coffin Ed said.

"It sounded like more than eleven shots to me," the bartender contended.

"That's when you ducked," Grave Digger said disappointedly, figuring the account was finished,

"That's when I should have ducked," the bartender admitted. "Everybody else ducked. But I ran to the front of the bar, trying to get Snake Hips' attention and call him inside, as if he hadn't heard all that shooting more than I did. But you don't know what you're thinking at a time like that. So I stood there waving my arms while the man in the car ducked out of sight. The white man had fell flat on his stomach when the shooting started, and I don't think he was hit then, I wasn't really looking, although I could see him from where I stood; but I was looking at the car, and he must have shot back at the man in the car because I saw two bullet holes suddenly appear in the right-front window."

"Now we're getting somewhere," Coffin Ed said.

"Check," Grave Digger echoed.

"I was still trying to get Snake Hips' attention," the bartender admitted. "But he was scared blind. He was just standing there with his arms straight up and his hands shaking like leaves. He was trembling all over and his coat was open, and I knew he must have been cold. I think he was saying—begging rather—for them not to shoot him—"

"Leave Snake Hips," Coffin Ed said brutally. "What about the other two?"

"Well, they must have begun shooting when the man in the car finished. Maybe they took advantage to get out their guns. When the shooting from the car stopped more shooting was still going on, and I looked over and saw flashes coming from both of their guns. Their pistols looked like the same kind of snub-nosed pistol the man had on the ground. One of them was shooting from his right hand and the other from his left—"

"The white man the lefty?"

"No, sir, it was the colored man. He had his sap in his right hand and was shooting from his hip—"

"From his hip?" Grave Digger said.

"Yes, sir, like a real Western gunman—"

"Hollywood style," Coffin Ed said scornfully.

"Let him go on," Grave Digger snapped.

"The white man had the brief case in his left hand, and he was shooting with his right hand held straight out in front of him like the man on the ground had done—"

"He's the son," Coffin Ed muttered.

"Was either of them hit?" Grave Digger asked.

"I don't think so. I don't think the man on the ground ever got a chance to shoot at them. After the man in the car had finished shooting they opened up; or they might have even opened up before he finished shooting. Anyway, the man on the ground never had a chance."

"And you were standing there watching all the time?" Grave Digger asked.

"Yes, sir, like a fool. I saw when Snake Hips was hit. At least I knew he was hit because he went straight down. He didn't fall like they do in the motion pictures; he just collapsed. I don't know who shot him, of course; but it was one of them up there beside Mr. Holmes, because the man in the car had quit shooting by then. I figure it was the white man who shot him, because he was the one who was holding his pistol so high."

"Don't you believe it," Coffin Ed said. "That son wasn't throwing bullets that wide apart."

"His number came up, and that's that," Grave Digger said. "And you didn't see the man on the ground catch his."

"Next time I noticed him he was just lying there like he had gone to sleep on his stomach, but to tell you the truth, sir, I wasn't paying him no attention especially. I was waiting for the three cops—heistmen I mean—to leave so I could go out and get Snake Hips. Then when they did leave I thought what was the use—he was dead; I knew he was dead when he went down; then I remembered I wasn't supposed to move a dead body. So I just stood there."

"And even then you didn't call the police," Coffin Ed accused.

"No, sir."

"What in the hell were you doing, then? Hiding when it was all over?"

The bartender lowered his eyes. When his voice came it was so low they had to lean forward to hear it. "I was crying," he confessed.

For a moment neither Grave Digger nor Coffin Ed had anywhere to look.

Then Grave Digger asked, in a voice unnecessarily harsh, "Did you see the license of the Buick, by any chance?"

The bartender got himself under control. "I didn't exactly look at it, I mean make a point of it—looking at it, I mean; then I couldn't see it too well; but it clicked in the back of my mind that it was a Yonkers number."

"How did you notice that?"

"I live in Yonkers, and I was thinking it was fate that the car carrying the murderers of Snake Hips came from the place where I live."

"Goddammit, let's bury Snake Hips," Coffin Ed said roughly. "Give us a description of the two men who got out of the car."

"You're asking me more than I can do, sir. I really didn't look at their faces. Then the orange neon light from the bar sign was shining on them, and that makes faces look different from what they actually are; so I hardly ever look at faces outside. All I know is one man was black—"

"Not half black?"

"No, sir, all black. And the other one was white."

"Foreign."

"It didn't strike me that way. I'd say Southern. Something about him reminded me of one of those Southern deputy sheriffs—sort of slouching when he moved, but moving faster than what it looked, and strong. Something sort of mean-looking about him, sadistic, I'd say. The kind of man who thinks just being white is everything."

"Not the kind who'd be welcome in here," Grave Digger said.

"No, sir. The fellows would be scared of him."

"But not whores?"

"Whores, too. But they'd take his money just the same. And he might be the kind who'd spend it on cheap whores."

"All right, describe the car."

"It was just a plain black Buick. About three years old, I'd say offhand. Plain black tires. Just the ordinary lights, as far as I saw. I wouldn't have noticed it if it hadn't been for them."

"And they drove off toward Eighth Avenue?"

"Yes, sir. Then people came from everywhere. A man came in here from Blumstein's and telephoned the police. And that's all I know."

"It's been like pulling teeth," Grave Digger said.

"All right, get on your coat and hat—you're going to the station," Coffin Ed said.

The bartender looked shocked. "But I thought—"

"And you can put down that glass before you wear it out."

"But I thought if I told you everything I saw—I mean—you're not arresting me, are you?"

"No, son, you're not being arrested, but you got to repeat your story for the Homicide officers and for the record," Grave Digger said.

Outside, the experts had itemized the material clues. The Assistant Medical Examiner had been and gone. He hadn't disclosed anything that wasn't obvious.

An examination of the white stiff's clothes had revealed that he was an operative for the Pinkerton Detective Agency.

"It won't take long to check with the New York office and find out his assignment. That will tell us something," the Homicide lieutenant said. "What did you boys find out?"

"Just what could be seen without knowing what it meant," Grave Digger said. "This is the bartender; he saw it all."

"Fine. We'll get it down. Too bad you didn't have a stenographer with you."

"We might not have got what we did," Coffin Ed said. "No one talks freely when it's being taken down."

"Anyway, you got it in your heads, if I know you two," the Homicide lieutenant said. "As soon as they move these stiffs, we'll all get together in the precinct station and correlate what we got." He turned to the precinct lieutenant, Anderson. "What about those bar jockeys? You want any more of them?"

"I'm having a man take their names and addresses," Anderson said. "I'll go along with Jones and Johnson on the witness they picked."

"Right," the lieutenant said, beating the cold from his gloved hands and looking up and down the street. "What's happening to those dead wagons?"

6

On his radio, Anderson got a call to come in. The bored voice of the switchboard sergeant informed him that the prowl car sent up to the convent reported a corpse, and asked what he wanted done.

Anderson told him to order the car to stay put and he'd send the Homicide crew up there.

The Homicide lieutenant ordered one of his detectives to call the Assistant Medical Examiner again.

Haggerty said, "Old Doc Fullhouse ain't going to like spending his nights in Harlem with bodies as cold as these."

Anderson said, "You go along with Jones and Johnson; I'll take the witness back to the station in my car."

Grave Digger and Coffin Ed, with Haggerty in back, led the Homicide car down 125th Street to Convent Avenue and up the hill to the south side of the convent grounds.

The prowl car was parked by the convent wall in the middle of the block. There was not a pedestrian in sight.

The three cops were sitting inside their car to keep warm, but they jumped out and looked alert when the Homicide car drew up.

"There it is," one of them said, pointing toward the convent wall. "We haven't touched anything."

The corpse was flattened against the wall in an upright position, with its arms hanging straight down and its feet raised several inches from the pavement. It was entirely covered, except for the head, by a long, black, shapeless coat, threadbare and slightly greenish, with a moth-eaten, rabbit-fur collar. The hands were encased in black, knitted mittens; the feet in old-fashioned, high-buttoned shoes that had recently been cleaned with liquid polish. The face seemed to be buried in the solid concrete, so that only the back of the head was visible. Glossy waves of black, oily hair gleamed in the dim light.

"Holy Mary! What happened here?" the Homicide lieutenant exclaimed as the group of detectives pressed close.

Flashlights came into play, lighting the grotesque figure.

"What is it?" a hardened Homicide detective asked.

"How does it stick there?" another wondered.

"It's a bad joke," Haggerty said, "it's just a dummy, frozen to the wall."

Grave Digger groped at a leg through folds of garments. "It ain't no dummy," he said.

"Don't touch it until the M. E. gets here," the Homicide lieutenant cautioned. "It might fall."

"It looks like it might be garroted," one of the cops from the prowl car offered.

The Homicide lieutenant turned on him with a face suddenly gone beet-red. "Garroted! From within the convent? By who, the nuns?"

The cop backtracked hastily. "I didn't mean by the nuns. A gang of niggers might have done it."

Grave Digger and Coffin Ed turned to look at him.

"It's just a way of speaking," the cop said defensively.

"I'll take a look," Grave Digger said.

He stood on tiptoe and peered down the back of the fur collar.

"Nothing around its neck," he said.

While still on tiptoe, he sniffed the wavy hair. Then he blew into it softly. Strands of silky hair floated outward. He dropped to his feet.

The lieutenant looked at him questioningly.

"Anyway, she's no grandma," Grave Digger said. "Her hair looks like a job from the Rose Meta beauty parlors."

"Well, let's see what's keeping her up," the lieutenant said.

They discovered an iron bar protruding from the wall at a point about six feet high. Below and above it there were deep cracks in the cement; and, at one point above, the crack had been dug out to form a long, oblong hole. The face of the corpse had been thrust into this hole with sufficient force to clamp it, and the end of the bar was caught between the legs, holding it aloft.

"Jesus Christ, it looks like it's been hammered in there," the lieutenant said.

"They're no signs of bruises on the back of the head," Grave Digger pointed out.

"One thing is for sure," Haggerty cracked. "She didn't get there by herself."

"You're going to be a senator someday," the lieutenant said.

"Maybe she was hit by a car," a harness cop suggested.

"I'll buy that," Coffin Ed said.

"Hit by a car!" the lieutenant exclaimed. "Goddammit, she'd have to be hit by a car traveling like a jet plane to get rammed into that wall like that."

"Not necessarily," Grave Digger said.

The flip cop said, "Oh, I forgot—there's a wig in the gutter across the street."

The lieutenant gave him a reproving look, but didn't say the words.

In a group, they trudged across the street. The cold east wind whipped at them, and their mouths gave off steam like little locomotives.

It was a cheap wig of gray hair, fashioned in a bun at the back, and it was weighted down by a car jack.

"Was the jack with it?" the lieutenant asked.

"No, sir—I put the jack on it to keep the wind from blowing it away," the cop replied.

The lieutenant moved the jack with his foot and picked up the wig. A detective held a light.

"All I can say about it is it looks like hair," the lieutenant said.

"Looks like real nigger hair," the flip cop said.

"If you use that word again I'll kick your teeth down your throat," Coffin Ed said.

The cop bristled. "Knock whose teeth—"

He never got to finish. Coffin Ed planted a left hook in his stomach and crossed an overhand right to the jaw. The cop went down on his hips; his head leaned slowly forward until it stopped between his knees.

No one said anything. It was a delicate situation. Coffin Ed was due a reprimand, but the lieutenant from Homicide was the ranking officer, and the cop had already riled him with the crack about the nuns.

"He asked for it," he muttered to himself, then turned to the other prowl-car cop. "Take him back to the station."

"Yes, sir," the cop said with a dead-pan expression, giving Coffin Ed a threatening look.

Grave Digger put a hand on Coffin Ed's arm. "Easy, man," he murmured.

The cop helped his partner to his feet. He could stand, but he was groggy. They got in the prowl car and drove off.

The others recrossed the street and stared at the corpse. The lieutenant stuck the wig into his overcoat pocket.

"How old would you say she was?" he asked Grave Digger.

"Young," Grave Digger said. "Middle twenties."

"What beats me is *why* would a young woman masquerade as an old woman *for*?"

"Maybe she was trying to impersonate a nun," a Homicide detective ventured.

The lieutenant began to turn red. "You mean so she could get into the convent?"

"Not necessarily—maybe she had a racket."

"What kind of racket?" The lieutenant looked at Grave Digger as though he had all the answers.

"Don't ask me," Grave Digger said. "Folks up here are dreaming up new rackets every day. They got the time and the imagination, and all they need is a racket to make the money."

"Well, all we can do now is leave her for Doc Fullhouse," the lieutenant said. "Let's go over the ground and see what it tells."

Grave Digger got a heavy flashlight from the glove compartment of their car, and he and Coffin Ed walked back to the intersection.

The others covered the area nearer to the corpse. No tire marks were evident where a car might have braked suddenly; they found no broken glass.

Coming up the street from Convent Avenue, playing the light from right to left, Grave Digger noticed two small black marks on the gray-black asphalt, and they knelt in the street to study them.

"Somebody gunned a car here," he concluded.

"I'd say a big car with a used tread, but we'll leave it for the experts."

Coffin Ed noticed a car with a wheel jacked up. On closer inspection they noticed that the opposite wheel was missing. They looked at one another.

"That's the money," Grave Digger said.

"For this one," Coffin Ed agreed. "Some local tire thief witnessed the kill."

"What he saw made him broom like the devil was after him."

"If he wasn't seen and taken away."

"Not that son. He had presence of mind enough to get away with his wheel," Grave Digger said.

"He oughtn't to be hard to find. Any son out tire-thieving on a night like this has got some pretty hot skirt to support."

The lieutenant listened to their findings with interest but no particular concern.

"What I want to know is how this woman got killed," he said. "Then we'll know what to look for."

A car turned in from Convent Avenue, and Coffin Ed said, "We ought to soon know; that looks like Doc's struggle-buggy."

Doctor Fullhouse was bundled up as though on an expedition to the South Pole. He was an old, slow-moving man, and what could be seen of his face between an astrakhan cap and a thick yellow cashmere muffler made one think of a laughing mummy.

His spectacles steamed over the instant he stepped from his overheated car, and he had to take them off. He peered about from watery blue eyes, searching for the body.

"Where's the cadaver?" he asked in a querulous voice.

The lieutenant pointed. "Stuck to the wall."

"You didn't tell me it was a vampire bat," he complained.

The lieutenant laughed dutifully.

"Well, get it down," Doc said. "You don't expect me to climb up there and examine it."

Grave Digger clutched one arm, Coffin Ed the other; the two detectives from Homicide took a leg apiece. The body was stiff as a plaster cast. They tried to move it gently, but the face was firmly stuck. They tugged, and suddenly the body fell.

They laid the corpse on its back. The black skin of the cheeks framing the cockscomb of frozen blood had turned a strange powdery gray. Drops of frozen blood clung to the staring eyeballs.

"My God!" one of the Homicide detectives muttered, stepped to the curb and vomited.

The others swallowed hard.

Doc got a lamp from his car with a long extension cord and focused the light on the body. He looked at it without emotion.

"That's death for you," he said. "She was probably a good-looking woman."

No one said anything. Even Haggerty's tongue had dried up.

"All right, give me a hand," Doc said. "We got to undress her."

Grave Digger lifted her shoulders, and Doc peeled off the coat.

The other detectives got off her gloves and shoes. Doc cut open the thick black dress with a pair of shears. Underneath she wore only a black uplift bra and lace-trimmed nylon panties. Her limbs were smooth, and well-rounded, but muscular. Falsies came off with the bra, revealing a smooth, flat, mannish chest. Underneath the nylon panties was a heavily padded, yellow satin loincloth.

Grave Digger and Coffin Ed exchanged a quick, knowing glance. But the others didn't get it until the loincloth had been cut and stripped from the hard narrow hips.

"Well, I'll be God-damned!" the Homicide lieutenant exclaimed. "She's a man!"

"There ain't any doubt about that," Haggerty said, finding his voice at last.

Doc turned the body over. Across the back, at the base of the spine, was a tremendous welt, colored dark grape-purple.

"Well, that's what did it," Doc said. "He was struck here by great force and catapulted into the wall."

"By what, for chrissake?" the lieutenant asked.

"Certainly not by a baseball bat," Haggerty said.

"My conjecture is that he was hit by an automobile from behind," Doc ventured. "I couldn't say positively until after the autopsy; and maybe not then."

The lieutenant looked from the street to the convent wall. "Frankly, Doc, I don't believe he was knocked from the street against that wall in the position that we found him," he said. "Isn't there a possibility that he was run over and then stuck up there afterwards?"

Doc made a bundle of the clothes, covered the body with its coat and stood up.

"Everything is possible," he said. "If you can imagine a driver running over him, then stopping his car and getting out and propping the body against the wall, and pushing its face into that crevice until it was stuck, then—"

The lieutenant cut him off. "Well, goddammit, I can imagine

that better than I can imagine the body being knocked up there from the street, no matter what hit it. Besides which, people have been known to do things worse than that."

Doc patted him on the shoulder, smiling indulgently. "Don't try to make your job any harder than it is," he said. "Look for a hit-and-run driver, and leave the maniacs to Bellevue's psychiatrists."

7

It was past two o'clock Sunday morning. Sand-fine sleet was peppering the windshield of the small black sedan as it hustled down the East Side Drive. There was just enough heat from the defroster to make the windshield sticky, and a coating of ice was forming across Grave Digger's vision.

"This heater only works in the blazing hot summer," he complained. "In this kind of weather it just makes ice."

"Turn it off," Coffin Ed said.

The car skidded on a glazed spot on the asphalt, and from the back seat Detective Tombs from Homicide Bureau yelled, "Watch it, man! Can't you drive without skidding?"

Grave Digger chuckled. "You work with murder every day, and here you are—scared of getting scratched."

"I just don't want to wind up in the East River with a car on my back," Tombs said.

The witness giggled.

That settled it. Conversation ceased. They didn't want outsiders horning in on their own private horseplay.

When they drew up before the morgue downtown on 29th Street, they all looked grim and half-frozen.

An attendant sitting at a desk in the entrance foyer checked them in, recording their names and badge numbers.

The barman from the Paris Bar gave his name as Alfonso Marcus and his address as 217 Formosa Street, Yonkers, N.Y.

They walked through corridors and downstairs to the "cold room." Another attendant opened a door and turned on a switch.

He grinned. "A little chilly, eh?" he said, getting off his standard joke.

"You ain't been outside, son," Coffin Ed said.

"We want to see the victim of a hit-and-run driver from Harlem," Grave Digger said.

"Oh yes, the colored man," the attendant said.

He led them down the long, bare room, lit by cold, white light, and glanced at a card on what looked like the drawer of a huge filing cabinet.

"Unidentified," he said, pulling out the drawer.

It rolled out smoothly and soundlessly. He removed a coarse white sheet covering the body.

"It hasn't been autopsied yet," he said, adding with a grin, "got to take its turn like everybody else. It's been a busy night—two asphyxiations from Brooklyn; one ice pick stabbing, also from Brooklyn; three poisonings, one by lye—"

Grave Digger cut him off. "You're holding us spellbound."

Coffin Ed took the bartender by the arm and shoved him close.

"My God," the bartender whimpered, covering his face with his hands.

"Look at it, goddammit!" Coffin Ed flared. "What the hell you think we brought you down here for—to start gagging at the sight of a stiff?"

Despite his horror, the bartender giggled.

Grave Digger reached over and pulled his hands from his face.

"Who is he?" he asked in a flat, emotionless voice.

"Oh, I couldn't say." The bartender looked as though he might burst out crying. "Jesus Christ in heaven, look at his face."

"Who is he?" Grave Digger repeated flatly.

"How can I tell? I can't see his face. It's all covered with blood."

"If you come back in an hour or two they'll have it all cleaned up," the morgue attendant said.

Grave Digger gripped the bartender by the back of his neck and pushed his head toward the nude body.

"Goddammit, you don't need to see his face to recognize him," he said. "Who is he? And I ain't going to ask you no more."

"He's Black Beauty," the bartender whispered. "What's left of him."

Grave Digger released him and let him straighten up.

The bartender shuddered.

"Get yourself together," Grave Digger said.

The bartender looked at him from big, pleading eyes.

"What's his square moniker?" Grave Digger asked.

The bartender shook his head.

"I'm giving you a chance," Grave Digger told him.

"I really don't know," the bartender said.

"The hell you don't!"

"No, sir, I swear. If I knew I'd tell you."

The morgue attendant looked at the bartender with compassion. He turned toward Grave Digger and said indignantly, "You can't third-degree a prisoner in here."

"You can't help him," Grave Digger replied. "Even if you are a member of the club."

"What club?"

"Let's take him out of here," Coffin Ed said.

Detective Tombs listened to the byplay with fascination.

They took the witness outside to their car and put him in the back seat beside Detective Tombs.

"Who's Mister Baron?" Grave Digger asked.

The bartender turned pleadingly to the white detective. "If I knew, sir, I'd tell them."

"Don't appeal to me," Tombs said. "Half of this is Greek to me."

"Listen, son," Coffin Ed said to the bartender. "Don't make it hard on yourself."

"But I just know these people from the bar, sir," the bartender contended. "I don't know what they do."

"It's going to be just too bad," Grave Digger said. "What you don't know is going to hang you."

Again the bartender appealed to the white detective. "Please, sir, I don't want to get mixed up in all this bad business. I've got a wife and family."

The windows of the small, crowded car had steamed over. The face of the detective couldn't be seen, but his embarrassment was tangible. "Don't cry to me," he said harshly. "I didn't tell you to get married."

Suddenly the bartender giggled. Emotions exploded. The white detective cursed. Grave Digger banged the metal edge of his hand against the steering wheel. The muscles in Coffin Ed's face jumped like salt on a fresh wound as he reached across the back of the seat and double-slapped the bartender with his left hand.

Grave Digger rolled down a window.

"We need some air in here," he said.

The bartender began to cry.

"Give me a fill-in," the white detective said.

"The one who got killed in the heist and the one we just saw are newlyweds," Grave Digger said. "This one"—he nodded toward the bartender—"is Snake Hips' used-to-be."

"How did you dig that?"

"Just guessing. They're all just one big club. But you got to know it. It's like when I was in Paris at the end of the war. All of us colored soldiers, no matter what rank or from what army or division, belonged to the same set. We all hung out at the same joints, ate the same food, told the same jokes, laid the same poules. There wasn't anything that one of us could do that the whole God-damned shooting party didn't know about."

"I see what you mean. But what's the angle here?"

"We haven't guessed that far," Grave Digger admitted. "Probably none. We're just trying to get all these people in position. And this one is going to help us. Or he's going to get something even he can't handle."

"Not before I get done with him," the detective said. "My boss man wants him to look at some pictures in the gallery. Maybe he can identify the heistmen—one of them at least."

"How long do you think that will take?" Coffin Ed asked.

"A few hours, maybe, or a few days. We can't employ your techniques; all we can do is keep him looking until he goes blind."

Grave Digger mashed the starter. "We'll take you down to Centre Street."

The detective and his witness got out in front of the Headquarters Annex, a loft building across the street from the domed headquarters building.

Coffin Ed leaned out of the window and said, "We'll be waiting for you, lover."

By the time they got back uptown, the windshield was frosted over with a quarter-inch coating of ice. Approaching headlights resembled hazy spectrums coming out of the sea.

They had a new dent in their right fender and a claim against their insurance company from the irate owner of a chauffeur-driven Rolls Royce whom they had attempted to pass on a stretch of slick ice just north of the U.N. Building.

Coffin Ed chuckled. "He was mad, wasn't he."

"Can you blame him?" Grave Digger said. "He felt the same as Queen Elizabeth would if we tramped into Buckingham Palace with muddy feet."

"Why don't you turn off that heater? You've said yourself it don't make nothing but ice."

"What, and catch pneumonia!"

They had been tippling a bottle of bourbon, and Grave Digger felt sort of witty.

"Anyway, you might slow down if you can't see," Coffin Ed said.

"It's nights like this that cause wars," Grave Digger philosophized without slacking speed.

"How so?"

"Increases the population. Then when you get enough prime males they start fighting to kill them off."

"Look out for that garbage truck!" Coffin Ed cried as they turned on two wheels into 125th Street.

"Is that what that was?" Grave Digger asked.

It was past three o'clock. They worked a special detail from eight until four, and this was the hour they usually contacted stool pigeons.

But tonight even stool pigeons had gone under cover. The 125th Street railroad station was closed and locked, and next door the all-night cafeteria was roped off except for a few tables at the front, occupied by bums clinging to bone-dry coffee cups and keeping one foot moving to prove they weren't asleep.

"Going back to the case, or rather cases—the trouble with these people is they lie for kicks," Grave Digger said seriously.

"They want to be treated rough; brings out the female in them," Coffin Ed agreed.

"But not too rough; they don't want to lose any teeth."

"That's how we're going to get them," Coffin Ed summed up.

Lieutenant Anderson was waiting for them. He had taken over the captain's office, and was mulling over reports.

He greeted them, as they came in bunched up and ashy from cold, with: "We got a line on the private eye who was killed. Paul Zalkin."

Coffin Ed backed up against the radiator, and Grave Digger perched a ham on the edge of the desk. The rough whisky humor was knocked out of them, and they looked serious and intent.

"Casper talk?" Grave Digger asked.

"No, he's still in a coma. But Lieutenant Brogan got through to the Pinkerton Agency and got a fill-in on Zalkin's assignment. The secretary of the national committee of Holmes' party stopped by his office earlier last night and left him fifty grand in cash, for organizational expenses for the presidential election this fall. Holmes hinted that he might take the money home with him rather than leave it in his office safe over the weekend. You know he lives in one of those old apartment houses on 110th Street, overlooking Central Park."

"We know where he lives," Coffin Ed said.

"Well, the secretary got to thinking about it after he had left, so he called the Pinkerton Agency and asked them to send a man up to cover Holmes on his way home. But he didn't want Holmes to think he was spying on him, so he asked that the man keep out of sight. That's how come Zalkin was there when the heist was staged."

"How long was it before the secretary left Casper?" Grave Digger asked, frowning with an idea.

"The agency got the call at ten-twenty o'clock."

"Then somebody knew about the payoff beforehand," Grave Digger said. "You can't organize a heist like that in that length of time."

"Not even in a day," Coffin Ed said. "These men were pros; and you can't get pros like ordering groceries. They might have had their uniforms, but they'd have to lift a car—"

"It hasn't even been reported as stolen yet," Anderson cut in.

"I got a notion these guns were from out of town," Coffin Ed went on. "No local hoods would choose 125th Street for a caper like that. Not that block of 125th Street. They couldn't depend on the weather to drive the ground hogs in their holes; and normally on a Saturday night that block, with all its bars and restaurants, would be jumping with pedestrians. They had to be somebody who didn't know this."

"That doesn't help us much," Anderson said. "If they're from out of town, they're long gone by now."

"Maybe," Grave Digger said. "Maybe not. If it wasn't for this hit-and-run business, I might buy it."

Anderson gave him a startled look.

"What the hell, Jones; you can't think there's a tie-in."

Coffin Ed grunted.

"Who knows," Grave Digger said. "There is something specially vicious about both those capers, and there ain't that many vicious people running loose in Harlem on a night as cold as this."

"My God, man, you can't think that hit-and-run was done deliberately."

"And then in both instances pansies were croaked," Grave Digger went on. "Accidents just don't happen to those people like that."

"The hit-and-run driver couldn't have possibly known his victim was a man," Anderson argued.

"Not unless he knew who he was and what racket he was pulling," Grave Digger said.

"What racket was he pulling?"

"Don't ask me. It's just a feeling I got."

"Hell, man, you're going mystical on me," Anderson said. "How about you, Johnson. Do you go along with that?"

"Yep," Coffin Ed said. "Me and Digger have been drinking out the same bottle."

"Well, before you get too drunk with that mysticism, let me fill you in with the latest facts. The two patrolmen, Stick and Price, who thought it was a joke to report they'd been knocked down by a homemade flying saucer, have admitted they were hit by a runaway automobile wheel coming down Convent Avenue. Does that give you any ideas?"

Grave Digger looked at his watch. It said five minutes to four.

"Not any that won't keep until tomorrow," he said. "If I start talking to my old lady about automobile tires, as fat as she's getting, I'm subject to losing my happy home."

8

When Roman came to the castle standing in the fork, where St. Nicholas Place branches off from St. Nicholas Avenue, he stood on the brake.

Sassafras sailed headfirst into the windshield, and Mister Baron's unconscious figure rolled off the back seat and plumped onto the floor.

"Which way did they go?" Roman asked, reaching for the .45 revolver that lay on the seat between them.

Sassafras straightened up, rubbing her forehead, and turned on him angrily. "You asking me? I ain't seen which way they went. They might have went downtown for all I know."

"I seen them turn uptown," he argued, his cocked gray eyes seeming to peer down both streets at once.

"Well, make up your mind," she said in her high, keening voice. "They didn't go into the castle, that's for sure. And you can't set here in the middle of the street all night."

"I wish I had the mother-raper who built that castle there in the middle of Harlem," Roman said as though it were responsible for his losing sight of the Cadillac.

"Well, you ain't got him, and you better get out the middle of the street before someone comes along and claims you has stolen this Buick."

"We has, ain't we?" Roman said.

The bump had revived Mister Baron, and they could hear him groaning down on the floor behind them. "Oh God . . . Oh Jesus Christ . . . Those dirty bastards . . ."

Roman slipped the car in gear and drove slowly down between the rows of brick-fronted apartment buildings on St. Nicholas Place.

The castle, somebody's brainstorm at the turn of the century, stood at 149th Street; above were the better-class residences for the colored people of Harlem. Roman was unfamiliar with this part of town, and he didn't know which way to turn.

Mister Baron gripped the back of the front seat and pulled himself to his knees. His long, wavy hair hung down over his forehead; his eyes rolled loosely in their sockets.

"Let me out," he said, moaning. "I'm going to be sick."

Roman stopped the car in front of a red brick building with a fluted façade. Big new cars lined the curbs.

"Shut up!" he said. "If it hadn't been for you, I never would have run off after hitting that old lady."

Mister Baron's mouth ballooned, but he held it back. "I'm going to be sick in the car," he blubbered.

"Let him out," Sassafras said. "If you'd listened to me, none of this would have happened."

"Get out, man," Roman shouted. "You want me to lift you?"

Mister Baron opened the curbside door and polled to his feet. He staggered groggily toward a lamppost. Roman jumped from the other side and followed him.

Mister Baron clung to the post and heaved. Steam rose as though he were spouting boiling water. Roman backed away.

"Jesus Christ in heaven," Mister Baron moaned.

Roman let him finish and clutched him by the arm. Mister Baron tried weakly to free himself.

"Let me go—I got to make a phone call," he said.

"You ain't going nowhere until I find my car," Roman muttered, pushing him toward the Buick.

Mister Baron pulled back, but he could scarcely stand. His head was filled with shooting pains, and his vision wouldn't focus. "Fool, how can I help you find your car if you won't let me telephone? I want to call the police and report that it's been stolen." His voice sounded desperate.

"Naw, you don't; you ain't telling the police nothing," Roman said, pushing him into the back of the car and slamming the door. He went around the car and climbed back beneath the wheel. "You think I want to get arrested?"

"Those weren't real police, you idiot," Mister Baron said.

"I know they weren't police. You think I'm a fool? But what am I going to tell the sure enough police about hitting that old lady?"

"You didn't hurt that old lady. I looked back once when you were driving off and saw her getting up."

Roman stared at Mister Baron while that sunk in. Sassafras turned about to look at Mister Baron, too. The two of them, suddenly staring and immobile—he with his Davy Crockett coonskin cap and she with the tasseled red knitted cap topping her long, black face—looked like people from another world.

"You knew I didn't hurt her, and you kept egging me to run away." Roman's thick Southern voice sounded dangerous.

Mister Baron fidgeted nervously. "I was going to stop you, but before I could say anything those bandits drove up and took advantage of the situation."

"How do I know you ain't in with 'em?"

"What for?"

"They stole my car. How do I know you ain't had 'em do it?"

"You're a fool," Mister Baron cried.

"He ain't such a fool," Sassafras said.

"Fool or not, I'm going to hold on to you until I find my car," Roman told Mister Baron. "And, if I don't find it, I'm going to take my money 'way from you."

Mister Baron started laughing hysterically. "Go ahead and take it. Search me. Beat me up. You're big and strong."

"I worked a whole year for that money."

"You worked a whole year. And you saved up sixty-five hundred dollars—"

"That's nearmost every penny I made. I went without eating to save that money."

"So you could buy a Cadillac. You weren't satisfied with an ordinary Cadillac. You had to buy a solid gold Cadillac. And I'm the—the—I'm the one who sold it to you. For a thousand dollars less than list price. Ha ha ha! You had it twenty minutes and let somebody steal it—"

"What's the matter with you, man? You going crazy?"

"Now you want your money back from me. Ha ha ha! Go ahead and start hitting me. Take it out of my skin. If that don't satisfy you, throw me down and rape me."

"Look out now, I don't go for that stuff."

"You don't go for that stuff. You goddam chicken-crap square."

"You're going to make me hit you."

"Hit me! Come on and hit me." Mister Baron thrust his womanish face toward Roman's lowering scowl. "See if you can knock sixty-five hundred dollars out of me."

"I don't have to. I can just throw you down and take it."

"Throw me down and take it! Wouldn't I love that!"

Sassafras put in her bit. "You ain't going to love what he's going to take 'cause it's just going to be money."

"Goddammit, where were you two squares when those bandits knocked me out and robbed me?" Mister Baron asked.

"Knocked you out?" Roman said stupidly.

"Is that what was the matter with you?" Sassafras echoed.

"And they robbed you? Of my money?"

"It was my money," Mister Baron corrected. "The car was yours, and the money was mine."

"Jesus Christ," Roman said. "They took the car and the money."

"That's right, square. Are you going to let me go and make that phone call now?"

"Naw, I ain't. I going to take you out and search you. I might be a square, but I ain't trusted you from the start."

"That's fine," Mister Baron said, and started to get out onto the sidewalk.

But Roman reached back, grabbed him and forced him out into the street. Then he got out and started shaking him down.

"Be careful, Roman," Sassafras said. "Somebody might come by here and think you is robbing him."

"Let 'em think what they want," Roman said, turning Mister Baron's pockets inside out.

"Do you want me to undress?" Mister Baron asked.

Roman finished with his pockets and felt through his clothes; then ran his hands over Mister Baron's body, up and down his legs and underneath his arms.

"He ain't got it on him," he conceded.

But he wasn't satisfied. He searched the back of the Buick.

"It ain't there, either." He took off his coonskin cap and rubbed his short, curly hair back and forth. "If I catch those mother-rapers I going to kill 'em," he said.

"Let him telephone," Sassafras said. "He said you ain't hurt the old lady, and I is ready to swear you ain't even hit her."

Roman stood in the street, thinking it over. Mister Baron stood beside him, watching his expression.

"All right, get in the car," Roman said.

Mister Baron got back into the car.

Roman began talking through the window. "You know this neighborhood—"

"Get in the car yourself," Sassafras said.

He got back into the front seat and continued addressing Mister Baron. "Where would they likely go with my car? It ain't like as if they could hide it."

"God only knows," Mister Baron said. "Let the police find it; that's what they get paid for."

"Let me give it some thought," Roman said.

"How much thought you going to give it?" Sassafras said.

"I tell you what," Roman said. "You go and phone the police and tell 'em it's your car. Then, if they find it, I'll show 'em my bill of sale."

"That's fine," Mister Baron said. "Can I get out now?"

"Naw, you can't get out now. I'm going to take you to a telephone, and when you get through talking to the police we're going to keep on looking ourselves. And I ain't going to let you go until somebody finds it."

"All right," Mister Baron said. "Just as you say."

"Where is there a telephone?"

"Drive down the street to Bowman's Bar."

He drove down to the end of St. Nicholas Place. Edgecombe Drive circles in along the ridge of the embankment overlooking Broadhurst Avenue and the Harlem River valley, and cuts off St. Nicholas Place at the 155th Street Bridge. Below, to one side of the bridge, is the old abandoned Heaven of Father Divine with the faded white letters of the word PEACE on both sides of the gabled roof. Beyond, on the river bank, is the shack where the hood threw acid into Coffin Ed's face that night three years ago, when he and Grave Digger closed in on their gold-mine pitch.

One side of Bowman's was a bar, the other a restaurant. Next to the restaurant was a barbershop; up over the bar was a dance hall. All of them were open; a crap game was going in back of the barbershop, a club dance in the hall upstairs. But not a soul was in sight. There was nothing in the street but the cold, dark air.

Roman double-parked before the plate-glass front of the bar. Venetian blinds closed off the interior.

"You go with him, Sassy," he said. "Don't let him try to get away with nothing."

"Get away with what?" Mister Baron said.

"Anything," Roman said.

Sassafras accompanied Mister Baron into the bar. Roman couldn't tell which one of them swished the more. He was looking through the right-side window, watching them, when suddenly he noticed two bullet holes in the window. He had been in the Korean war and learned the meaning of the sudden appearance of bullet holes. He thought someone was shooting at him, and he ducked down on the seat and grabbed his pistol. He lay there for a moment, listening. He didn't hear anything, so he peered cautiously over the ledge of the door. No one was in sight. He straightened up slowly, holding the pistol ready to shoot if an enemy appeared. None appeared. He looked at the bullet holes more closely and decided they had been there all along. He felt sheepish.

It occurred to him that someone in the car had been in a gunfight. No doubt those phony cops. He turned about to examine the other side to see where the bullets had gone. There were two holes about a foot apart in the ceiling fabric above his head. He got out and looked at the top. The bullets had dented it but hadn't penetrated. They must be in the lining of the ceiling, he thought.

He turned on the inside light and looked about the floor. He found seven shiny brass jackets of .38 caliber cartridges sprinkled over the matting.

It had been some fight, he thought. But the full meaning didn't strike him right away. All he could think of at the moment was how those bastards had taken his car.

He put his pistol back on the seat beside him and sat there picking his nose.

Two cops in a prowl car with the lights out slipped quietly up beside him. They were on the lookout for that particular car. But when they saw him, sitting there in his coonskin cap, looking as unconcerned as though he were fishing for eels underneath the bridge, they didn't give the car a second glance.

"One of the Crocketts," the driver said.

"Don't wake him," the other replied.

The car slipped noiselessly past. He didn't see it until it had pulled ahead.

Trying to catch some whore hustling, he thought. Motherrapers come along and steal my car and all these cops can do is chase whores.

The bar ran lengthwise, facing a row of booths. It was crowded. People were standing two and three deep.

Sassafras went ahead of Mister Baron, elbowing through the jam. She stopped and turned around.

"Where is the phones?"

"In the restaurant," Mister Baron said. "We have to go all the way to the back."

"You go ahead," she said, pulling aside so he could pass.

A joker on a bar stool reached out and tugged the tassels of her cap.

"Little Red Riding Hood," he cooed. "How about you."

She snatched her cap from his hand and said, "How about your baby sister?"

The man drew back in mock affront. "I don't play that."

"Then pat your feet," she said.

The man grinned. "What you drinking, baby."

Her glance had caught the smoky oil paintings of two brownskin amazon nudes reclining on Elysian fields above the mirror behind the bar. She tried not to laugh, but she couldn't help it.

The man followed her glance. "Hell, baby, you don't need much as what they got."

She gave herself a shake. "At least what I got moves," she said.

Suddenly she remembered Mister Baron. She started off. The man grabbed her by the arm.

"What's the rush, baby?"

She tore herself loose and squeezed hurriedly to the rear. Glass doors opened into the restaurant, and she bumped into a waitress going through. The phone booth was to the rear on the left. The door was closed. She snatched it open. A man was phoning, but it wasn't Mister Baron.

"'Scuse me," she said.

"Come on in," the man said, grabbing at her.

She jerked away and looked about wildly. Mister Baron was nowhere in sight.

She stopped the waitress coming back.

"Did you see a little prissy man with wavy hair come through here?" she asked.

The waitress looked her over from head to feet.

"You that hard up, baby?"

"Oh shoo you!" she cried and dashed through the swinging doors into the kitchen.

"Did a man come through here?" she asked.

The big, sweating, bald-headed cook was up a tree.

"Git out of here, whore!" he shouted in a rage.

The dishwasher grinned. "Come 'round to the back door," he said.

The cook grabbed a skillet and advanced on her, and she backed through the doorway. She looked through the dining room and bar again, but Mister Baron had disappeared.

She went outside and told Roman, "He's gone."

"Gone where?"

"I don't know. He got away."

"Where in the hell was you?"

"I was watching him all the time, but he just disappeared."

She looked like she was about to cry.

"Get in the car," he said. "I'll look for him."

She took her turn sitting in the hottest car in all of New York State while he searched the bar and restaurant for Mister Baron. He didn't have any better luck with the cook.

"He must have got out through the kitchen," he said when he returned to the car.

"The cook would have seen him."

"It'd take a shotgun to talk to that evil man."

He climbed in behind the wheel and sat there looking dejected. "You let him get away, now what us going to do?" he said accusingly.

"It ain't my fault that we is in this mess," she flared. "If you hadn't been acting such a fool right from the start might not none of this happened."

"I knew what I was doing. If he'd tried to pull off something crooked, I was trying to trick him by making him think I was a square."

"Well, you sure made him," she said. "Asking do it use much gas and then looking at the oil stick and saying you guessed the motor was all right."

He defended himself. "I wanted all those people who was watching us to know I was buying the car so they could be witnesses in case anything happened."

"Well, where is they now? Or has some more got to happen?"

"Ain't no need of us arguing between ourselves," he said. "We got to do something."

"Well, let's go see a fortune teller," she said. "I know one who tells folks where to find things they has lost."

"Let's hurry, then," he said. "We got to get rid of this car 'fore daylight. It's hotter than a West Virginia coke oven."

9

Grave Digger and Coffin Ed were buttoning up their coats when the telephone rang in the captain's office.

Lieutenant Anderson took the call and looked up. "It's for one of you."

"I'll take it," Grave Digger said and picked up the receiver. "Jones speaking."

The voice at the other end said, "It's me, Lady Gypsy, Digger."

He waited.

"You're looking for a certain car, ain't you? A black Buick with Yonkers plates?"

"How do you know that?"

"I'm a fortune teller, ain't I?"

Grave Digger signaled Coffin Ed to cut in, and jiggled the hook.

Coffin Ed picked up one of the extensions on the desk and Lieutenant Anderson the other. The switchboard operator knew what to do.

"Where is it?" Grave Digger asked.

"It's sitting as big as life down on the street in front of my place," Lady Gypsy said.

Grave Digger palmed the mouthpiece and whispered an address on 116th Street.

Anderson picked up the intercom and ordered the sergeant on the switchboard to alert all prowl cars and await further instructions.

"Who's in it?" Grave Digger asked.

"Ain't nobody in it at the moment," Lady Gypsy said. "I got a square and his girl friend up here in my seance chamber who drove up in it. They got a wild story about a lost Cadillac—"

"Hold the story," Grave Digger said. "And keep them there, even if you have to use ghosts. Me and Ed will be there before you can say Jack Robinson."

"I'll send the cars on," Anderson said.

"Give us three minutes and seal off the block," Grave Digger said. "Have them come in quietly with the blinkers off."

Lady Gypsy's joint was on the second floor of a tenement on 116th Street, midway between Lexington and Third Avenues. On the ground floor was an ice and coal store.

The painted tin plaque in a box beside the entrance read:

Lady Gypsy
Perceptions—Divinations
Prophesies—Revelations
Numbers Given

The word *Findings* had been recently added. Business had been bad.

Once upon a time Lady Gypsy had lived an ultrarespectable private life in an old dark house on upper Convent Avenue with her two bosom associates: Sister Gabriel, who sold tickets to heaven and begged alms for nonexistent charities; and Big Kathy, who ran a whorehouse on East 131st Street. They were known in that upper-crust colored neighborhood as "The Three Black Widows." But when Sister Gabriel got his throat cut by one of the trio of con men responsible for the acid-throwing caper that permanently scarred Coffin Ed's face, the two remaining "Widows" let the house go, relinquished respectability and holed up in their dens of vice.

Now Lady Gypsy was seldom seen outside the junk-crammed five-room apartment where she contacted the spirits and sometimes gave messages to the initiate that were out of this world.

It was a normal five-minute drive on open streets from the 126th Street precinct station, but Grave Digger made it in his allotted three. Sleet blew along the frozen streets like dry sand, making the tires sing. The car didn't skid, but it shifted from side to side of the street, as though on a sanded spot of slick ice. Grave Digger drove from memory of the streets, with the bright lights on, more to be seen than to see, because sighting through his windshield was like looking through frosted glass. His siren was silent.

A prowl car was parked in front of Lady Gypsy's but no sign of the Buick.

"Anderson jumped the gun," Coffin Ed said.

"They might have got 'em," Grave Digger said without much hope.

The little car skidded when he tamped the brake, and it banged into the rear bumper of the prowl car. They hit the street without giving it a thought.

Coffin Ed went first, overcoat flapping, pistol in his hand. Grave Digger slipped as he was rounding the back of the car and hit the top of the luggage compartment with the butt of his pistol. Coffin Ed wheeled about to find Grave Digger rising from the gutter.

"You're sending telegrams," Coffin Ed accused.

"It ain't my night," Grave Digger said.

A prowl car rounded the distant corner, siren wide open and red eye blinking.

"Makes no difference now," Coffin Ed said disgustedly, taking the dimly lit stairs two at a time.

They found a uniformed cop standing beside the door at the head of the staircase with a drawn pistol, another in the shadows of the stairs, leading to the upper floors.

"Where's the car?" Coffin Ed asked.

"There wasn't any car," the cop said.

Grave Digger cursed. "What are you doing here?"

"Lieutenant said to seal up this joint and wait for you."

"What's going to stop them from going out the back?"

"Joe and Eddie got the back covered."

Grave Digger couldn't hear him over the screaming of the siren down below.

"How's the back?" he shouted.

"Covered," the cop shouted back.

"Well, let's see what gives," Grave Digger said.

The siren died to a whimper, and his voice filled the narrow corridor like organ notes.

"Hold it!" a voice cried from below.

Two cops pounded up the stairs like the Russian Army.

"This beats vaudeville," Coffin Ed said.

The cops came into sight with guns in their fists. They halted at sight of the assemblage, and both turned bright pink.

"We didn't know anybody was here," one of them said.

"You were making sure just in case," Coffin Ed said.

Grave Digger fingered the buzzer beside the door. From inside came the distant sound of a bell ringing.

"These doorbells always sound like they're miles away," he said.

The cops looked at him curiously.

No one came to the door.

"Let me shoot the lock off," a cop said.

"You can't shoot these locks off," Grave Digger said. "Look at them; there are more locks on this door than on Fort Knox and there're more inside."

"There's a chance that only one is locked," Coffin Ed said. "If somebody left here who didn't have a key—"

"Right," Grave Digger agreed. "I'm too tired to think."

A cop raised his eyebrows, but Grave Digger didn't see it.

"Stand back," Coffin Ed said.

Everyone backed off to one side.

He backed to the opposite wall, leveled his long-barreled .38 and put four bullets about the Yale snap lock. Sound shattered the front hall windows, and doors down at the back of the hall cracked open an inch. From all directions came the sound of a sudden scurrying like rats deserting a ship.

"Let's hit it," Coffin Ed said, coughing slightly from the cordite fumes filling the hall.

The sound of scurrying ceased.

He and Grave Digger hit the door with left shoulders, and reeled into a room.

It was a reception room. Decrepit kitchen chairs flanked opposite walls. A stained, dusty, dark-blue, threadbare carpet covered the floor. In the center, a round table-top seemed to be floating in the air. It was supported by four small steel cables, which, attached to the ceiling, were practically invisible in the dim light. On the table rested a gruesome-looking sepulcher made of dull-gray papier-mâché. Out of this sepulcher was coming the ghost of Jesus Christ.

Coffin Ed caught himself, but Grave Digger reeled into the hanging table with such force that he overturned the sepulcher and the ghost of Christ went sailing across the room as though the devil had grabbed at it.

The uniformed cops followed, looking from one to the other with wide-eyed consternation.

Someone started hammering on the back door. Another bell starting ringing.

"Pipe down!" Grave Digger shouted.

The noise ceased.

The walls of the room were papered with faded blue skies packed with constellations. Across from the entrance was a double doorway closed by a faded red curtain containing the gilded signs of the zodiac.

Coffin Ed stepped over the ghost of Christ and parted the zodiac.

They found themselves in the seance chamber. A crystal ball sat on a draped table. All four walls were curtained in some kind of dark satiny material covered with luminescent figures of stars, moons, suns, ghosts, griffins, animals, angels, devils, and faces of African witch doctors.

The room was lit by a faint glow from the crystal ball. Their sudden entrance stirred the curtain to fluttering, and the luminescent figures flickered in and out of sight.

"Where the hell's the light?" Grave Digger roared. "I'm getting seasick."

A cop flashed on his torch. They didn't see another light.

"Let's find the doors," he said, tearing the curtains aside.

Behind the curtains there were doors everywhere.

He opened the first one that gave. It led to a dining room. A chandelier with four bulbs lit a square dining room table covered with a black-and-silver checked plastic cloth. Two chairs were drawn up to two dirty plates and the skeleton of a roasted opossum, lying one-sided in congealed possum grease and the remains of baked yellow yams, like the ribs of a derelict ship in shallow surf.

"Possum and taters," Coffin Ed said, unconsciously licking his lips.

"That's what they ate, but where are they?" Grave Digger said.

"Ain't nobody here but us ghosts," a cop said.

"Don't forget us possums," another added.

Coffin Ed opened another door and found himself in a kitchen. He heard movement on the outside open-air stairs.

"Hey, let us in," a voice called from without.

A cop pushed past Coffin Ed to open the back door.

Grave Digger had opened another door, which led to a bedroom. "In here," he called.

Coffin Ed went in, and six cops followed.

A fat, light-complexioned colored man with a flabby, sensual face and a shining, bald head lay across the bed, breathing heavily with his eyes closed. He wore a big, old-fashioned faded-yellow brassiere, holding his lopping breasts, and a pair of purple-and-golden striped boxer shorts, from which extended the fasteners of a worn garter belt attached to the tops of purple silk stockings. He was fat, but his flesh was so flabby it spread out beside his bones like melted tallow.

Another bald-headed man lay face down on the floor beside the bed. He wore a red-and-gray striped rayon bathrobe over white-dotted blue rayon pyjamas. His face was unseen, but the fringe of hair beneath his bald dome was silky white.

The white cops stared.

"What did they do with Lady Gypsy?" one asked.

"That's him on the bed," Coffin Ed said.

"That ain't the question," Grave Digger said. "We got to find out who it was slugged him."

"He isn't talking," a white cop said.

"We'll fix that," Grave Digger said. "Get a bottle of vinegar from the kitchen."

He reached over and clutched Lady Gypsy by the arm and pulled him over to the side of the bed. Then, when the cop brought the vinegar, he opened the bottle and poured the lukewarm liquid over Lady Gypsy's face.

"That the way you do it?" the cop asked.

"It works," Grave Digger said.

"Every time," Coffin Ed supplemented.

Lady Gypsy stirred and spluttered. "Who is that pissing on me?" he said in a distinct, cultivated voice.

"It's me, Digger," Grave Digger said.

Lady Gypsy sat up suddenly on the side of the bed. He opened his eyes and saw all the white cops staring at him.

"You sonofabitch," he said.

Grave Digger slapped him with his left hand.

His head fell to one side and straightened up as though his neck were made of rubber.

"It wasn't my fault the bastard got away," he said, fingering an egg-size lump on the back of his head. He looked down at his half-naked self. "He took my second-best ensemble."

"Fill us in," Grave Digger said. "And don't start begging for sympathy."

Lady Gypsy flipped back the covers and wiped his face with the top end of the sheet. "He's a rough boy," he said. "A square, but really ragged." There were threads of desire and admiration in his voice. "And he's carrying a rusty forty-five."

"If you go patsy on me, I'll kick out your teeth," Grave Digger said.

Again the white cops looked at him curiously.

"You don't have any compassion for anybody," Lady Gypsy said in his cultivated voice.

"It's how you look at it," Grave Digger said. He turned to Coffin Ed. "Get out your stop watch, Ed. I'm going to give him ninety seconds."

Lady Gypsy regarded him impassively through glazed, yellow-speckled brownish eyes that had the slight blue cast of age.

"You are an animal," he said.

Grave Digger hit him in the mouth. It made a sound like water splashing, and blood drops spurted from the corners of Lady Gypsy's mouth. But his big, flaccid body didn't move, and his flat, stoical expression went unruffled.

"I'm not scared of you, Digger," he said. "But I'm going to tell you what I know because I don't want to get beat up." He wiped the blood from his bruised and swelling lips with the vinegary sheet end. "You're forgetting it was me who tipped you."

"Yeah, and you let him sap you and get away while you was making a pass at him," Grave Digger accused.

"That's not so. He followed me in here and heard me phoning." He nodded toward the telephone on the night table. "Not that I wouldn't have if I had known what was coming," he added.

"Forty seconds," Coffin Ed said.

"He worked for a year as an able-bodied seaman for the South American Shipping Line." He spoke steadily but unhurriedly. "On the SS *Costa Brava.* Saved all his money. Bought a new Cadillac from a man called Mister Baron—"

"Baron again," Grave Digger said, exchanging looks with Coffin Ed.

"Paid six thousand, five hundred for it," Lady Gypsy went on unemotionally. "Got it for a thousand dollars under the list price. A Cadillac with a golden finish—"

The white cops' mouths had come open.

"He had just paid the money and got his bill of sale, and he was taking it for a tryout when he hit an old woman—"

"Alongside the convent?"

Lady Gypsy flicked him an upward look, then dropped his gaze and stared at nothing again.

"Then you know about it?"

"You tell us."

"I'm just telling you what he told me—"

The man on the floor stirred slightly and moaned.

"Won't you put Mister Gypsy on the bed," Lady Gypsy said.

"Let him lay where he is," Grave Digger said.

"So they hit this old lady and ran," he went on tonelessly. "They didn't get far before they were stopped by three men in cops' uniforms driving a Buick—"

"It begins to click," Grave Digger said.

"Check," Coffin Ed replied.

Lady Gypsy told the rest of the story in the same toneless voice. "Then, when Mister Baron got away, they came to me," he concluded. "They wanted me to tell them where to find the Cadillac."

"Did you tell them?" a white cop asked, eyes popping.

"If I could do that I wouldn't be living in this dump," Lady Gypsy said. "I'd be riding in a yacht on the Riviera."

The man on the floor groaned again, and two white cops lifted him and laid him across the foot of the bed.

"How did he know about you?" Grave Digger asked.

"He didn't. His girl friend told him. Brought him, rather."

"Who is she?"

"Sassafras Jenkins. A girl on the town."

"Did she steer him into Baron?"

"He doesn't think so. He said he met Mister Baron at the docks in Brooklyn—where the Line has their warehouse. On his last trip in, two months ago. Mister Baron gave him a lift into Harlem; he was driving his own Cadillac convertible. Roman told him he was saving up his money to buy a car, and Mister Baron asked him how much he had saved, and he said he'd have six thousand, five hundred dollars when he came back from his next trip and Mister Baron said he'd get him a Cadillac convertible like the one he was driving for that amount—"

"He was driving a gold-finished Cadillac himself?"

"No, his was gray. But he asked Roman what color he wanted, and Roman said he wanted one that looked like solid gold."

"What was Baron's business in Brooklyn?" Grave Digger asked.

"Sailors, Digger," Coffin Ed said. "Where's your thinking cap?"

Grave Digger half agreed. "Maybe, maybe not. Maybe he was fishing frogs for snakes."

"It's the same thing," Coffin Ed contended. "Sailors are everything to everybody."

"You know Baron?" Grave Digger said to Lady Gypsy.

"It happens that I don't."

"You know Black Beauty."

"Yes."

"What was his racket?"

"Pimping."

"Pimping! That pansy!"

"You said his racket, not his pleasure. And you employed the past tense. Is he dead?"

"He was the old woman who got killed."

"Killed? They said she wasn't hurt."

"That's another story. But you must know Baron. He's in the clique."

"That's what I told myself," Lady Gypsy admitted. "But truthfully, I don't."

"You know the Jenkins girl, however."

Lady Gypsy shrugged. "I've seen her. I don't know her. She comes in here from time to time with various tricks. She's always got some little racket going."

"With Baron?"

"You can't trick me, Digger. I've told you the truth about Mister Baron. I don't know him, and I don't think she knew him, either."

"Okay! Okay! Where do we find her?"

"Find *her*? How would I know where to find a chippie whore?"

"You got *Findings* written on your board downstairs," Coffin Ed put in.

"Yeah, and you'd better live up to it or you are going to find yourself where you don't want to be found," Grave Digger added.

"You know that old courtyard between One-eleventh and One-twelfth Streets?"

"The Alley."

"Yes. She's got a man in one of those holes in there somewhere."

"Who's the man?"

"Just a man, Digger. I don't know who he is or what he does. You know I wouldn't be interested in a man who was interested in a chippie like that."

"Okay, Ed, let's get going," Grave Digger said.

"We'd better call the desk first and let Anderson know the horse got out."

"You call him."

Coffin Ed reached for the telephone on the night table.

Grave Digger turned to the cops and said, "You men had better get back to your cars; you've been off the street too long as it is."

Lady Gypsy said, "I want to put in a charge against that man for assault and battery and theft."

"You'll have to go to the station," Grave Digger said. "And you had better wear a suit."

10

When Roman and Sassafras came running down the stairs from Lady Gypsy's and made for the Buick parked at the curb, it was a good thing that nobody saw them. They were enough to catch the eyes of the blind. Roman had stuck Lady Gypsy's fortune-telling turban, with its big glass eye, on the side of his head—so now he had three eyes all looking in different directions. He had draped the rainbow-colored gown over his leather jumper and army pants, but it was too short, and his paratrooper boots were showing. He carried his coonskin cap in his left hand and his big rusty .45 in his right. "If we get caught I'm going to act crazy and start running," he panted hoarsely. "They won't shoot a crazy fortune teller."

Sassafras started giggling.

Roman gave her a dirty look as he ran around and climbed in behind the wheel. He put his pistol and coonskin cap on the seat between them and took off in a hurry. But some sixth sense told him he had a better chance of getting away by driving slowly.

He was driving like a preacher on the way to church when he came to Third Avenue and turned south.

The occupants of the first of the prowl cars coming fast from the north saw the slow-moving Buick just before the prowl car screamed around the corner into 116th Street. They didn't give it a second thought. They hadn't seen the driver, and they couldn't imagine anybody crawling along at that speed in the hottest car east of the Mississippi River.

Roman drove down past 114th Street and parked in front of a mattress factory behind an open-bed truck.

"I got to give this situation some thought," he said.

Sassafras couldn't stop giggling. Every time she looked at him it got worse.

"This ain't no laughing time," he said hoarsely. "You're going to make me mad."

"I know it ain't, sugar," she admitted, half choking. "But ain't nobody looking at you in that get-up going to burst out crying."

"Well, it's your fault," he accused. "Taking me to see that stool pigeon—"

"How was I to know he was a stool pigeon," she flared. "I been there lots of times before with other mens and he ain't never—" She caught herself.

"I know you has," he said. "You don't have to rub it in. I ain't expected you to get all rusty while I've been away. I ain't no fool."

She put her arm about his neck and tried to pull his head down to her. "I has been true to you, sugar," she said. "I swear it on a stack of Bibles."

He pulled his head back. "Listen, baby, this ain't no time for sweet talk. Here I is, done blowed a whole year's pay, and you is swearing to bald-face lies on stacks of Bibles."

"It ain't no lie," she said. "If you'd taken the trouble to test it, instead of buying Cadillacs—"

"You wanted the car as much as me."

"What if I did? That don't mean I think a Cadillac is the only thing God made."

"This ain't no time to argue," he said. "We has got to do something—and fast. I got a notion we has been awfully lucky so far, but it ain't going to last forever. The cops is going to catch us in this hot car and then—"

She cut him off. "We could go see a man I know who's in the automobile business. He might can help us."

"I done seen all the men in the automobile business I needs to see," he said. "I has had it. What I'm thinking of doing is see if I can find some of my ship-buddies and get them to help me look for my car."

"This man I'm talking about could do more good than them," she contended. "If that big bright Cadillac is anywhere in Harlem, he is more likely to find it than anybody I know of."

"If all these mens you know—" he began, but she wouldn't let him finish.

"What mens?"

"This bald-headed pappy passing himself off as a fortune teller—"

Her lips curled. "You ain't jealous of him, I hope."

"Well, he damn sure wasn't no woman."

"This man ain't a bit like him."

"If you think that makes me happy—"

"It ain't like that," she said. "I hardly know him. He's just a business acquaintance."

"What kind of business?"

But she ignored that. "We can ask him to look around and see what he might find," she said. "And also we can stay in his house whilst he's looking. You ain't got nowhere to stay."

"I was depending on staying with you the time I wasn't staying in my car. Is you got some man staying in your room?"

"You make me sick," she said. "You know can't no man stay in my room, as respectable as those people is I room with."

"Well, how is us going to pay this man for staying in his house and searching for our car?" he wanted to know. "I gave Mister Baron my last dollar."

"We can sell him the tires off this car," she said. "He's in the used-tire business."

"I get it," he said. "I ain't as dumb as you think. He's a tire thief."

"Well, what if he is," she said. "He's got to know where cars is at in order to steal their tires. And that's just who you need, somebody who knows something."

"Well, all right then, let's go give him the tires off this car and get started looking. Where is he at?"

"He lives in the Alley. He's got a big place of his own."

He started the car and drove down to 112th Street and turned back toward Lexington. Just back of the buildings facing on Third Avenue was a narrow passageway that turned at a right angle and ran between the crosstown streets.

It was a tight squeeze for a big car—there wasn't space on either side to open the door and get out—and he had to back up three times to turn the corner.

"I'd hate to get caught in here," he said. "Ain't no way to go but up."

The Alley was flanked by rows of two-story brick buildings, in varying degrees of decay, that had once been carriage houses for the residents of 112th and 111th Streets. Now families lived on the second floors that had been servants quarters, and the carriage stalls were filled with long-forgotten junk, in which rats bred and children played and little girls lost their maidenheads.

"It's here," she said, indicating a rotten wooden carriage-house door spotted with patches of rusty tin. "Let me see if he's in."

The door was fastened by iron bars bolted to the rotten wood and a brass lock the size of a hitching block.

He stopped the car, and she got out and peered through a spyhole beside the lock.

"He ain't in," she said. "His motorcycle ain't here."

"What's us going to do?" he said.

"Let me think," she said, putting the tips of her mittened fingers to a dusty gray cheek and looking absent. "Oh!" she said brightly. "That reminds me. He gave me a key to the door."

She started digging in her handbag.

"What's he doing giving you a key to his door?" he asked suspiciously.

"It's for his girl friend," she said lightly. "She and I is pals. And he said if she come by and he was out for me to let her in."

To the right of the carriage-house doors was a small door that opened on to a staircase leading to the quarters above. She inserted a key in the Yale lock and said, "There! Now we can just go inside and wait for him."

"You know this man mighty well," he said.

"His girl friend and me is just like that," she said, holding up a hand with the thumb pressed tightly to the first mittened finger. "I'll just run up and get the key to the big lock so you can put the car inside where won't nobody see it."

"If I likes this, I likes oats in my ice cream," he said. "And I ain't no mule."

But she didn't wait to hear him. She ran up, got the key and opened the big doors, and he maneuvered the car into a dark, damp room with bare beams and a flagstoned floor smelling of tire rubber and earth mold. Hanging to toolboards on the walls were the various equipment for changing and repairing tires, but no tires were in sight.

He got out, grumbling to himself. She closed and locked the gate, switching about with a bright, excited insouciance, as though her pants were crawling with seventeen thousand queen ants.

"Now we'll just go upstairs and wait," she said, moving as though all the ants were biting her lightly.

The upstairs was one room. There were sets of windows at both back and front, the panes covered with oiled brown paper. In the center, on one side, was a coal-burning, potbellied stove. The nearest corner was filled by a double bed with a chipped, white-enameled iron frame. The opposite corner was curtained off for a clothes closet. On the other side of the stove was a chest of drawers with a cracked marble top, on which sat a two-burner gas plate. A square table with dirty dishes occupied the center of the floor. Before the inside windows was a third table with a cracked white porcelain washbowl and pitcher. Water was supplied by a hose coming from a single tap at the level of the baseboards. The toilet was outside, behind the carriage house. The only covering for the bare wooden floor was a variety of men's garments.

In addition to a single drop light in the center of the room, hanging from one of the uncovered beams were several tiny wall lamps from the ten-cent stores.

Sassafras turned on the bright drop light and flung her coat across the unmade bed. She was wearing a red knitted dress to match her cap, and black lace stockings.

It was so cold in the room their breath made vapor.

"I'm going to make a fire," she said. "You just set down and make yourself comfortable."

He gave her an evil and suspicious look, but she didn't notice it.

She bent over and looked into the potbellied stove, her duck-shaped bottom tightening the seat of her dress.

He put his coonskin cap on the table beside a dirty plate and placed the rusty pistol on top of it.

"There's a trap already laid," she said, and got a box of kitchen matches from the chest of drawers.

"You don't know where he keeps his money, too, do you?" he asked.

She lit the fire and opened the draft, then turned around and looked at him. "What're you grumbling about to yourself?"

"You're acting more at home here than a hen in a nest," he said. "You're sure your business with this man ain't what I'm thinking?"

She took off her cap and shook loose her short, straightened hair.

"Oh, don't be so jealous," she said. "You're frowning up enough to scare out the fire."

"I ain't jealous," he denied. "I'm just thinking."

She began clearing the dirty dishes from the table and stacking them beside the gas hot plate.

"You sailors is all just alike," she said. "If you had your way you'd handcuff a girl's legs together and take the key to sea."

"You ain't just saying it," he admitted, growing more and more angry as he watched her domestic activity.

The fire began roaring up the chimney, and she half-closed the damper. Then she turned and looked at him; her sloe eyes glittered like brilliants.

"Take off those Mother Hubbard clothes so I can kiss you," she said, shaking the kinks out of her muscles.

"This place sure is making you kissified," he complained.

"What's wrong with that?" she said. "You can't expect a cow to chew her cud when she got a field full of grass."

He glared at her. "If you make eyes at this man, there's going to be asses whipped," he said threateningly.

She moved into him and snatched off the turban with the third eye.

"That thing is galling your brains," she said.

"It ain't my brains," he denied.

"Don't I know it," she said, groping at him.

"Let me get off these womanish things," he said, and began pulling the robe up over his head. "I feels like a rooster trying to lay an egg."

"You is sure got chickens on your mind," she said, tickling him in the stomach while the robe covered his face.

He jumped back, laughing like a big tickled goon, hit his calves against the edge of the bed and fell sprawling across it on his back.

She jumped on top of him and tried to smother him with the folds of colored cloth. He tore open a hole for his head to come through, and she jumped backward to her feet and bent double laughing.

He got his feet on the floor and his legs underneath him, and pushed from the bed like a young bull starting a charge. His lips were stretched, his tongue lolled from one corner; he looked as though he might be panting, but his breath was held. The frown still knotted his forehead, but his gray eyes were lit, the right one focused on her and the left one ranging off in the direction of the stove. His head peered from the folds of colored cloth hanging across his leather jacket and down his back.

He lunged for her.

She let his hands touch her, then twisted out of his grip, spinning on her toes, and went half across the room.

He put his big shoulders low, long arms outstretched like a grappling wrestler, and charged toward her. She got the table in between them. She was panting with laughter.

"Butterfingers," she taunted, kicking off her shoes.

"I'll get you," he panted.

He knocked over a chair trying to circle the table, but she kept just beyond his reach. Then, with a quick unexpected motion, he gripped the table by the edge, lifted it inches from the floor and threw it to one side.

Now nothing stood between them.

She shrieked and turned, but he got hold of her waist from behind and rode her face down across the bed. She was lithe, quick, and strong, and she twisted from beneath him, coming face up at the foot of the bed. He jumped like a big cat and straddled her, gripping her upper arms with both hands.

She went limp for a moment and looked up at him from burning black challenging eyes. An effluvium of hot-bodied woman and dime-store perfume came up from her in a blast. It filled his mouth with tongue floating in a hot spring of saliva. Her lips were swollen, and her throat was corded. He could feel the hardness of her nipples through his leather jacket and woolen shirt.

"Take it and you can have it," she said.

Abruptly his mind began to work. His body went lax, his grip relaxed and his frown deepened.

"All this trouble I'm in and that's all you can think of," he said.

"If this won't cure your troubles nothing will," she murmured.

"We ain't got much time," he complained.

"If you're scared, go home!" she hissed, and balled herself up to jump from the bed.

He went taut again before she got away and flattened her shoulders back.

"I'm going to cool you off," he said.

She put her knees against his chest and pushed. He let go her arms and grabbed her stockinged legs just above the knees and began to open them. Her legs were strong enough to break a young man's back, and she put all of her strength into keeping them closed. But he hunched his overgrown muscles and began bearing down. They locked in a test of strength. Their breath came in gasps.

Slowly her legs began to open. They stared into one another's eyes. The stove had begun to smoke, and their eyes smarted.

Suddenly she gave way. Her legs went wide so quickly he fell on top of her. He clutched at flimsy cloth, and there was a tearing sound. He flung something from his hand. Buttons sailed in all directions, like corn popping.

"Now!" she screamed.

11

Three minutes after the Buick had squeezed into the Alley, a small black sedan skidded about the corner into 112th Street from Lexington Avenue.

Grave Digger was driving with the lights dimmed, and Coffin Ed was keeping a sharp lookout among the parked cars for the Buick.

The heater had suddenly begun to work, and the ice was melting on the windshield. The wind had shifted to the east, and the sleet had stopped. The tires sang softly in the shifting sleet on the asphalt street as the car straightened out; but the next moment it began going off to the right, so Grave Digger had to steer slightly left to keep it on a straight course.

"I got a feeling this is a wild-goose chase," Coffin Ed said. "It's hard to figure anybody being that stupid these days."

"Who knows?" Grave Digger said. "This boy ain't won no prizes so far."

They were halfway down the block of dilapidated old houses and jerry-built tenements when they spied a motorcycle with a sidecar turn into the other end from Third Avenue.

They became suddenly alert. They didn't recognize the vehicle; they knew nothing of its history, its use, or its owner. But they knew that anyone out on a night like that in an open vehicle bore investigation.

The rider of the motorcycle saw them at the instant they saw him. He saw a small black sedan coming crab-wise down the otherwise deserted street. As much trouble as he had gone to over the years to keep out of its way, he knew it like the plague.

He wore dark-brown coveralls, a woolen-lined army fatigue jacket, and a fur-lined, dark-plaid hunter's cap.

The seat had been removed from the sidecar, and in its place were two fully-tired automobile wheels covered with black tarpaulin.

When Coffin Ed spied the tarpaulin-covered objects, he said, "Do you see what I see?"

"I dig you," Grave Digger said, and stepped on the gas.

If the tires had been smaller, the rider would have swallowed them the way peddlers swallowed marijuana cigarettes when the cops closed in. Instead he gunned his motorcycle straight ahead, switching on the bright light to blind the two detectives, and leaning far over to the right side out of the line of fire. Motor roar filled the night like jet planes taking off.

Simultaneously Grave Digger switched on his bright lights. Coffin Ed had his pistol out and was fumbling with the handle to the window, trying to get it down. But he didn't have time.

The two vehicles roared straight toward one another on the half-slippery street.

Grave Digger tried to outguess him. He saw the joker leaning to his right, overtop the sidecar. He knew the joker had them figured to figure he'd be leaning to the left, balancing the sidecar for any quick maneuver. He cased the joker to make a sharp last-minute turn to the right, braking slightly to make a triangle skid, and try to pass the car on the left, on the driver's side, opposite the free-swinging gun of Coffin Ed.

So he jerked the little sedan sharply to the left, tamped the brakes and went into an oblique skid, blocking off the left side of the street.

But the joker outguessed Grave Digger. He made a rollover in his seat like a Hollywood Indian on a pinto pony, and broke a ninety-degree turn to his own left and gunned it to the limit for a flying skid.

His intention was to get past the sedan on the right side, and to hell with getting shot at.

Both drivers miscalculated the traction of the street. The hard, sleety coating was tricky; the tires bit in and gripped. The motorcycle sidecar hit the right-rear fender of the sedan at a tangent, and went into a full-gunned spin. The sedan wobbled on its rear wheels and threw Grave Digger off balance. The motorcycle went over the curb behind a parked car, bouncing like a rubber ball, bruised the rider's leg against a rusty iron stairpost and headed back in the direction it had come from.

Coffin Ed was stuck in the half-opened window, his gun arm pinioned and useless, shouting at the top of his voice: "Halt or I'll shoot!"

The rider heard him over the roar of the motor as he was fighting to keep the vehicle on the sidewalk and avoid sidescraping the row of stairposts on one side and the parked cars on the other.

The sedan was across the street, pointed at an angle toward the opposite curb, but headed in the general right direction.

"I'll get him," Grave Digger said, shifting back to first and tramping on the throttle.

But he hadn't straightened out the wheels from his sharp left turn, and, instead of the car curving back into the street, it bounded to the left and went broadside into a parked Chevy. The Chevy door caved in, and the left-front fender of the little sedan crumpled like tin foil. Glass flew from the smashed headlamp, and the rending sound of metal on metal woke up the neighborhood.

The thing to have done was to back up, straighten out and start over.

Grave Digger was so blind mad by this turn of events he kept tramping on the throttle and scraped past the Chevy by sheer horsepower. His own crumpled left-front fender caught in the Chevy's left-rear fender, and both broke loose from their respective cars.

He left them bouncing in the street and took off after the motorcycle that had bounced back into the street and was making a two-wheeled turn north up Third Avenue.

It was pushing four-thirty in the morning, and the big transport trucks were on the streets, coming from the west, through the tunnels underneath the Hudson River, and heading north through Manhattan Island toward upstate New York—Troy, Albany, Schenectady, or the Boston road.

A trailer truck was going north on Third Avenue when Grave Digger made the turn, and for a moment it looked as though he might go underneath it. Coffin Ed was leaning out the window with his pistol in his hand. He ducked back, but his gun was still in sight when they passed the driver's cabin.

The truck driver's eyes popped.

"Did you see that cannon?" he asked his helper.

"This is Harlem," his helper said. "It's crazy, man."

The white driver and the colored helper grinned at one another.

The motorcycle was taming west into 114th Street when Grave Digger got the sedan steadied from its shimmy. The melting ice on the windscreen was blurring his vision, and he turned on the wipers. For a moment he couldn't see at all. But he turned anyway, hoping he was right.

He bent too sharp and bumped over the near-side corner curb. Coffin Ed's head hit the ceiling.

"Goddam, Digger, you're beating me to death," he complained.

"All I can say is I've had better nights," Grave Digger muttered through clenched teeth.

They kept the motorcycle in sight until it turned north on Seventh Avenue, but didn't gain on it. For a time it was out of sight. When they came into Seventh Avenue, they didn't see it.

Three trucks were lined up on the outside lane, and a fourth was passing the one ahead.

"We don't want to lose that son," Grave Digger said.

"He's passing on the sidewalk," Coffin Ed said, leaning out his right-side window.

"Cut one over his head."

Coffin Ed crossed his left arm to overtop the window ledge, rested the long nickel-plated barrel atop his left wrist and blasted at the night. Flame lanced into the dark, and three blocks ahead a streetlamp went out.

The motorcycle curved from the sidewalk back into the street in front of the line of trucks. Grave Digger came up behind the truck on the inside lane and opened his siren.

At 116th Street Coffin Ed said, "He's keeping straight ahead. Trying to make the county line."

Grave Digger swerved to the left of the park that ran down between the traffic lanes and went up the left-hand side. The windshield wipers had cleared half-moons in the dirty glass, and he could see an open road. He pushed the throttle to the floor, gaining on the motorcycle across the dividing park.

"Slow him down, Ed," he said.

The park, circled by a small wire fence, was higher than the level of the street, and it shielded the motorcycle's tires. It was going too fast to risk shooting at the lamp. He threw three shots in back of it, but the rider didn't slow.

They passed two more northbound trucks, and for a time both lanes were clear. The sedan came up level with the motorcycle.

Coffin Ed said, "Watch him close, Digger, he's going to try some trick."

"He's as scared of these corners as we are," Grave Digger said. "He's going to try to crash us into a truck."

"He's got two up ahead."

"I'd better get behind him now."

At 121st Street Grave Digger swerved back to the right-side lanes.

One block ahead, a refrigerator truck was flashing its yellow passing lights as it pulled to the inner lane to pass an open truck carrying sheet metal.

The motorcycle rider had time to pass on the inside, but he hung back, riding the rear of the refrigerator truck until it had pulled clear over to the left, blocking both sides of the street.

"Get a tire now," Grave Digger said.

Coffin Ed leaned out of his window, took careful aim over his left wrist and let go his last two bullets. He missed the motorcycle tire with both shots, but the fifth and last one in his revolver was always a tracer bullet, since one night he had been caught shooting in the dark. They followed its white phosphorescent trajectory as it went past the rear tire, hit a manhole cover in the street, ricocheted in a slight upward angle and buried itself in the outside tire of the open truck carrying sheet metal. The tire exploded with a bank. The driver felt the truck lurch and hit the brakes.

This threw the motorcycle rider off his timing. He had planned to cut quickly between the two trucks and shoot ahead before the inside truck drew level with the truck it was passing. When he got them behind him the two trucks would block off the street, and he would make his getaway.

He was pulling up fast behind the car carrying sheet metal when the tire burst and the driver tamped his brakes. He wheeled sharply to the left, but not quickly enough.

The three thin sheets of stainless steel, six feet in width, with red flags flying from both corners, formed a blade less than a quarter of an inch thick. This blade caught the rider above his woolen-lined jacket, on the exposed part of his neck, which was stretched and taut from his physical exertion, as the motorcycle went underneath. He was hitting more than fifty-five miles an hour, and the blade severed his head from his body as though he had been guillotined.

His head rolled halfway up the sheets of metal while his body kept astride the seat and his hands gripped the handlebars. A stream of blood spurted from his severed jugular, but his body completed the maneuver, which his head had ordered and went past the truck as planned.

The truck driver glanced from his window to watch the passing truck as he kept braking to a stop. But instead he saw a man without a head passing on a motorcycle with a sidecar and a stream of steaming red blood lowing back in the wind.

He gasped and passed out.

His lax feet released the pressure from the brake and clutch, and the truck kept on ahead.

The motorcycle, ridden by a man without a head, surged forward at a rapid clip.

The driver of the refrigerator truck that was passing the open truck didn't believe what he saw. He switched on his bright lights, caught the headless motorcycle rider in their beam and quickly switched them off. He blinked his eyelids. It was the first time he had ever gone to sleep while driving, he thought; and my God, what a nightmare! He switched the lights back on, and there it still was. Man or hallucination, he was getting the hell away from there. He began flashing his blinkers as though he had gone crazy; he mashed the horn and stood on the throttle and looked to the other side.

The truck carrying the sheet metal turned gradually to the right from a faulty steering mechanism. It climbed over the shallow curb and started up the wide stone step of a big fashionable Negro church.

In the lighted box out in front of the church was the announcement of the sermon for the day.

Beware! Death is closer than you think!

The head rolled off the slow-moving truck, dropped to the sidewalk and rolled out into the street. Grave Digger, closing up fast, saw something that looked like a football with a cap on it bouncing on the black asphalt. It was caught in his one bright light, but the top was turned to him when he saw it, and he didn't recognize what it was. "What did he throw out?" he asked Coffin Ed. Coffin Ed was staring as though petrified. He gulped. "His head," he said.

Grave Digger's muscles jerked spasmodically. He hit the brake automatically.

A truck had closed in from behind unnoticed, and it couldn't stop in time. It smacked the little sedan gently, but that was enough. Grave Digger sailed forward; the bottom rim of the steering wheel caught him in the solar plexus and snapped his head down; his mouth hit the top rim of the steering wheel, and he mashed his lips and chipped two front teeth.

Coffin Ed went headfirst into the safety-glass windshield and battered out a hole. But his hard head saved him from serious injury.

"Goddam," Grave Digger lisped, straightening up and spitting out chipped enamel. "I'd have been better off with the Asiatic flu."

"God knows, Digger, I would have, too," Coffin Ed said.

Gradually the taut headless body on the motorcycle spewed out its blood and the muscles went limp. The motorcycle began to waver; it went to one side and then the other, crossed 125th Street, just missing a taxi, neatly circled around the big clock atop a post at the corner and crashed into the iron-barred door of the credit jewelry store, knocking down a sign that read:

We Will Give Credit to the Dead

12

Roman got up and fastened his belt.

"When is this joker coming?" He was all for business now.

Sassafras stood up and shook down her skirts. Her face was sweaty, and her eyes looked sleepy. Her dress was stretched out of shape.

"He ought to be here any time," she said, but she sounded as though she didn't care if he never came.

Roman began looking worried again. "You're sure this joker can help us? I've got a notion we're up against some rough studs, and I don't want nobody messing around who's going to get rattled."

Sassafras ran a greasy bone comb through her short, tousled hair. "Don't worry 'bout him," she said. "He ain't going to lose his head."

"This waiting around is dragging me," he said. "I wish we could do something."

"You call what we been doing nothing?" she said coyly.

"I mean about my car," he said. "It's going to soon be daylight and ain't nobody doing nothing."

She went over, put some coal on the fire and adjusted the damper. Her dress was pulled out of shape and hung one-sided.

"I'm going to see if he got any whisky left," she said, rummaging about the shoes on the floor of the curtained-off clothes corner.

He followed her and saw a green dress hanging with the men's clothes.

"This looks like your dress," he said suspiciously.

"Don't start that stuff again," she said. "You think they only made one dress when they made mine. Besides which, his girl friend is about the same size as me."

"You're sure she ain't wearing the same skin?" he said.

She ignored him. Finally she came up with a bottle of cheap blended whisky, three-quarters full.

"Here, drink this and shut up," she said, thrusting the bottle into his hands.

He uncorked it and let whisky gurgle down his throat. "It ain't bad, but it's mighty weak," he appraised.

"How you going to know bad whisky?" she said scornfully. "You've been drinking white mule all your life."

He took another drink, bringing the level down below half. "Baby, I'm hungry enough to eat a horse off his hoof and leave the skeleton still hitched to the plow," he said, flexing his muscles. "Why don't you see if your girl friend's boy friend has got anything to eat in this joint."

"If I found something, it'd just make you more suspicious," she said.

"Anyhow, it'd fill my belly."

She found some salt meat, a half loaf of white bread in wax-paper wrapping, and a bottle of molasses in the bottom drawer. Then she opened a back window and delved into a screened cold-box attached to the sill; she found a pot half-filled with congealed hominy grits and a frozen can of sliced California peaches.

"I don't see no coffee," she said.

"Who wants coffee?" he said, taking another swig from the bottle.

Shortly the room was filled with the delicious-smelling smoke of fried fat meat. She sliced the gelatinous hominy and browned it in the hot fat. He opened the can with his pocket knife but the contents were frozen solid, so he put the can on top of the stove.

She couldn't find but one clean plate, so she used one slightly soiled. She polished a couple of forks with a dry cloth.

He filled his plate with fried hominy, covered it with fried meat and doused it with molasses. He stuffed his mouth full of dry bread, then packed meat, hominy, and molasses on top of it.

She looked at him with disgust. "You can get the boy out the country, but you can't get the country out the boy," she philosophized, eating her meat daintily along with bites of bread and holding her fried hominy between the first finger and thumb, according to etiquette.

He was finished first. He got up and looked at the peaches. A core of ice still remained. He picked up the whisky bottle and measured it with his eye.

"You want some grog mixed with peach juice?" he asked.

She gave him a supercilious look. "I don't mind if I do," she said in a proper voice.

He looked about for a receptacle to hold the mixture, but not seeing any, he squeezed the rim of the can into a spout and poured the peach syrup into the whisky bottle. He shook it up and took a swallow and passed it to her. She took a swallow and passed it back.

Soon they were giggling and slapping at one another. The next thing they were on the bed again.

"I wish that man would hurry up and come on," he said, making one last effort to be sensible.

"What you want to go looking for an old Cadillac in this weather for, when here you is got me?" she said.

"Let's stop here and walk back," Coffin Ed said.

Grave Digger coasted to a stop beside the entrance to the Alley. It was a dark gray morning, and not a soul was in sight.

They alighted slowly, like decrepit old men.

"This jalopy looks as though it's been to the wars," Grave Digger lisped.

His lips were swollen to such proportions it looked as though his face were turning wrong side out.

"You look like you've been with it," Coffin Ed said.

"Yeah, let's hope there're no more jokers in this deck."

He started to lock the car doors and then saw the naked front wheel, the battered rear end, and the hole in the windshield, and he put the key into his pocket.

"We don't have to worry about anybody stealing it," he lisped.

"That's for sure," Coffin Ed agreed.

They picked their way along the uneven brick pavement, avoiding slick ice and stepping over frozen rats and cats. Garbage trucks couldn't get into the Alley, and residents piled their garbage in the street the year around. Now it presented an uneven pile of mounds along the walls of the carriage houses, composed chiefly of hog bones, cabbage leaves, and tin cans. They saw one lone black cat sitting on his haunches gnawing a piece of bacon rind frozen hard as a board.

"He must have stolen that," Coffin Ed said. "Nobody living in here has thrown that much good meat away."

"Let's go easy now," Grave Digger lisped.

When they came to the door, both took out their pistols and spun the cylinders. Brass bullets showed faintly against the gleaming nickel plate. Their shadowy figures had the silence of ghosts. They were mouth-breathing now, giving off soft puffs of vapor in the frigid air.

Grave Digger switched his pistol to his left hand and fished a key from his right overcoat pocket. As he fitted the key into the lock, Coffin Ed pulled hard on the knob. The Yale lock opened without a sound. Coffin Ed pushed the door in three inches, and Grave Digger withdrew the key.

Both flattened against the outside wall and listened. From above came sounds like two people sawing wood; a man sawing dry pine boards with a bucksaw and a boy sawing shingles with a toy.

Coffin Ed reached out and slowly pushed the door open with his pistol barrel. The two kept on sawing. He put his head around the doorframe and looked.

There was no door at the head of the stairs. The opening was lit by a soft pink light, revealing the naked beams of a ceiling.

Coffin Ed went up first, stepping on the outside edge of the stairs, testing each before putting down his weight. Grave Digger let him get five steps ahead and followed in his footsteps.

At the top, Coffin Ed stepped quickly into the pink light, his gun barrel moving from left to right.

Then without turning, he beckoned to Grave Digger.

They stood side by side looking at the sleeping figures on the bed.

The man wore a plaid woolen shirt, open all the way down and the shirttail out, a heavy-ribbed T-shirt, army pants, and stained white woolen socks. A leather jacket was piled on top of a pair of paratrooper boots on the floor beside the bed. He lay doubled up on one side, facing the woman, with an arm flung out across her stomach.

The woman wore a red knitted dress and black lace stockings. That seemed to be all. She lay half on her side, half on her back, with her legs outspread. Velvet black skin showed all the way up to her waist.

A single dim pink-shaded lamp hanging from a nail above the head of the bed made the scene look cozy.

Their gazes roved over the room, lingered on the big rusty .45 lying on the coonskin cap, went on and came back.

Coffin Ed tiptoed over and picked it up. He sniffed at the muzzle, shook his head and slipped it into his pocket.

Grave Digger tiptoed over to the bed and poked the sleeping man in the ribs with the muzzle of his own pistol.

Afterwards he admitted he shouldn't have done it.

Roman erupted from the bed like a scalded wildcat.

He came up all at once, all of him, as though released from a catapult. He struck a backhanded blow with his left hand while he was in the air, caught Grave Digger straight across his belly and knocked him on his rump.

Coffin Ed jumped over the top of Grave Digger's head and slashed at Roman with his pistol barrel.

But, while he was flat in the air, Roman doubled up and spun over, taking the blow on the fat of his hams and kicking Coffin Ed in the face with both stockinged feet.

Then the screaming began. It was high, loud, keening screaming that dynamited the brain and poured acid on the teeth. Sassafras had reared up on all fours and was kneeling in the bed with her mouth wide open.

Coffin Ed went back into the table. The legs splintered, and he crashed to the floor.

Roman landed on the flat of his shoulders and the palms of his hands while his feet were still in the air.

Grave Digger came up on his left hand, his left foot jackknifed beneath him, and tapped Roman across the top of the head with his pistol butt. But his flopping overcoat impeded the blow, and Roman gave no sign that he felt it. He doubled his feet beneath him and came up straight, like an acrobat, turning at the instant he touched floor.

Grave Digger backhanded with the same motion that tapped Roman on the head and hit his right kneecap. Roman went down on one side, like the pier of a house giving way. Coffin Ed staggered in and kicked him solidly in the left calf.

Sassafras's hair stood out like quills of a porcupine and her eyes were glazed, but the screaming kept on.

Roman fell into Grave Digger and clutched him by the leg, and, when Coffin Ed jumped forward to kick him away, he clutched his leg.

He got to his feet, holding each big man by a leg, and banged their heads into the ceiling beams.

"Run, Sassy, run!" he shouted. "This ain't no time for a fit."

She stopped screaming as suddenly as she had started. She jumped to her feet and started toward the door.

Grave Digger and Coffin Ed began raining pistol blows on Roman's head.

He sank to his knees but held on to their legs.

"Run, Sassy!" he gasped.

But she stopped at the doorway to run back and snatch up her new fur coat.

Grave Digger grabbed at her but missed.

"Turn loose, tough mouth!" Coffin Ed grated as he kept pounding Roman on the head.

But Roman held on long enough for Sassafras to scamper down the stairs like a frightened alley cat. Then he relaxed his grip; he grinned foolishly and murmured, "Solid bone . . ." He fell forward and rolled over.

Coffin Ed leaped toward the doorway, but Grave Digger called to him, lisping painfully, "Let her go. Let her go. He earned it."

13

It was eleven o'clock Sunday morning, and the good colored people of Harlem were on their way to church.

It was a gloomy, overcast day, miserable enough to make the most hardened sinner think twice about the hot, sunshiny streets of heaven before turning over and going back to sleep.

Grave Digger and Coffin Ed looked them over indifferently as they drove toward Harlem Hospital. A typical Sunday morning sight, come sun or come rain.

Old white-haired sisters bundled up like bales of cotton against the bitter cold; their equally white-haired men, stumbling along in oversized galoshes like the last herd of Uncle Toms, toddling the last mile toward salvation on half-frozen feet.

Middle-aged couples and their broods, products of the post-war generation, the prosperous generation, looking sanctimonious in their good warm clothes, going to praise the Lord for the white folks' blessings.

Young men who hadn't yet made it, dressed in lightweight suits and topcoats sold by color instead of quality or weight in the credit stores, with enough brown wrapping paper underneath their pastel shirts to keep them warm, laughing at the strange words of God and making like Solomon at the pretty brownskin girls.

Young women who were sure as hell going to make it or drop dead in the attempt, ashy with cold, clad in the unbelievable colors of cheap American dyes, some at that very moment catching the pneumonia, which would take them before that God they were on their way to worship.

From all over town they came.

To all over town they went.

The big churches and little churches, stone churches and storefront churches, to their own built churches and to hand-me-down churches.

To Baptist churches and African Methodist Episcopal churches and African Methodist Episcopal Zionist churches; to Holy Roller churches and Father Divine churches and Daddy Grace churches, Burning Bush churches, and churches of God and Christ.

To listen to their preachers preach the word of God: fat black preachers and tall yellow preachers; straightened-haired preachers and bald-headed preachers; family preachers and playboy preachers; men preachers and lady preachers and children preachers.

To listen to any sermon their preacher cared to preach. But on this cold day it had better be hot.

Grave Digger and Coffin Ed parked their wreck in front of the Harlem Hospital and went inside to the reception desk.

They asked to speak with Casper Holmes.

The cool, young colored nurse at the desk lifted a telephone and spoke some words. She put it down and gave them a cool, remote smile. "I am sorry, but he is still in a coma," she said.

"Don't be sorry for us, be sorry for him," Coffin Ed said.

Her smile froze as though the insect had talked back.

"Tell him it's Digger Jones and Ed Johnson," Grave Digger lisped.

She stared at the movement of his swollen lips with horrified fascination.

"Tell him we're just ahead of the Confederates," he went on. "Maybe that will get him out of his coma."

Her face twisted as though she had swallowed something disagreeable.

"Confederates," she murmured.

"You know who the Confederates are," Coffin Ed said. "They're the people who fought to keep us slaves."

She smiled tentatively to prove she wasn't sensitive about slavery jokes.

They stared at her, grave and unsmiling.

She waited and they waited.

Finally she picked up the telephone again and repeated their message to the floor supervisor.

They heard her say: "No, not conferees; they said *Con-fed-er-ates* . . . Yes . . ."

She put down the telephone and said without expression, "You will have to wait."

They waited; neither moved.

"Please wait in the waiting room," she said.

Behind them was a small nook with a table and several chairs, some occupied by others who were waiting.

"We'll wait here," Grave Digger lisped.

She pursed her lips. The telephone rang. She listened. "Yes," she said.

She looked up and said, "His room is on the third floor. Take the elevator to the right, please. The floor supervisor will direct you."

"You see," Grave Digger lisped. "You don't know what those Confederates are good for."

The room was banked with flowers.

Casper sat up in a white bed wearing a turban of white bandages. His broad black face loomed aggressively above yellow silk pajamas. He looked like an African potentate, but it wasn't a time for flattery.

French windows opened to a terrace facing the east. Two over-stuffed chairs ranged along one side of the bed. On the other side, remains of a breakfast littered a wheel tray. The detectives saw at a glance that it had been a substantial breakfast of fried sausage, poached eggs on toast, hominy grits with butter, fruit and cereal with cream, and a silver pot of coffee. A box of Havana cigars sat beside a basket of mixed fruit on the night stand.

The detectives took off their hats.

"Sit down, boys," Casper said. "What's this about Confederates?"

Grave Digger looked about for a window sill on which to rest a ham, was thwarted by the French window and compromised on the arm of a chair. Coffin Ed backed into a corner and leaned against the wall, his scarred face in the shadows.

"We were just kidding, boss," Grave Digger lisped. "We thought you might want to talk to us before the big brass from downtown gets up here."

Casper frowned. He didn't like the insinuation that he preferred talking to colored precinct detectives rather than to downtown white inspectors. But since he had tacitly admitted as much by seeing them, he decided to pass it.

"A God-damned embarrassing caper," he conceded. "Right in my own bailiwick."

Now he looked like a martyred potentate.

"That's what we figured," Coffin Ed said.

Casper flicked a quick, sly look from one to the other. "You must feel the same way," he observed. "Where were you at the time?"

"Eating chicken feetsy at Mammy Louise's," Grave Digger confessed.

Casper stared at him to see whether he was joking, decided he wasn't. He opened the box of cigars and selected one, picked up a gadget from the table and carefully snipped off the end, then reached for an imported gold lighter behind the box and snapped a flame. He applied the flame like a jeweler using a miniature torch on a filigree of gold, snapped shut the lighter, slowly rolled the end of the cigar about between his thick lips and blew out a thin stream of smoke. The good smell of fine tobacco dissipated the hospital odors.

As an afterthought, he extended the box toward the detectives. Both declined.

"I will tell you what I know, which isn't much," he said. "Then we will see what we can make out of it. You boys must have been working on it all night yourselves."

"Still at it," Grave Digger lisped.

"First we'll tell you what we got," Coffin Ed said. "A colored sailor, a country boy from Alabama, left his ship at about six o'clock last evening. He had been working for one entire year to save money to buy a car; when he got his final pay, he had six thousand, five hundred dollars in one-hundred-dollar bills in a money belt. The ship docks in Brooklyn. It was eight o'clock before he got uptown. He met his girl friend, Sassafras Jenkins. They had some drinks and then took a taxi over to an office on lower Convent Avenue, where he had an appointment to meet one Mister Baron, who was selling him the car."

Casper smoked his cigar softly, his black face impassive.

"The appointment was for ten o'clock," Coffin Ed went on. "Baron was a half hour late. He rode up in the car with a white man. Roman and his girl were waiting on the sidewalk in front of the dermatological clinic near One-twenty-sixth Street. The white man got out and went upstairs to an office in the rear. Roman and his girl stayed downstairs for another half hour with Baron, inspecting the car. A small crowd of people coming from the supermarket up the street collected.

"It was a brand-new Cadillac convertible with some kind of gold-like finish. Baron was selling it to Roman for six thousand, five hundred dollars."

Casper blinked but said nothing.

"You got a Cadillac convertible. What did yours cost?" Grave Digger asked.

"With accessories over eight thousand," Casper said.

"Roman paid six thousand, five hundred for his," Coffin Ed said. "The three of them went upstairs to the office where the white man was waiting, and executed the bill of sale. Sassafras witnessed it, and the white man signed as a notary public, using the name Bernard Kaufman. The white man left.

"Then the three of them took the car for a tryout at Baron's suggestion. He had Roman turn into the street south of the convent, where there would be little if any traffic, so he could test its pickup. Roman had no sooner started accelerating than he hit an old woman crossing the street. He wanted to stop, but Baron urged him to drive on. He didn't have any insurance; the car still had dealer's plates; he couldn't apply for registration until Monday morning; and he didn't have a driver's license. His girl friend didn't think the old woman was seriously hurt, but he ran anyway. He hadn't got clear of the block when a Buick drove up and forced him to a stop. Three men in police uniforms got out and accused him of hit-and-run manslaughter and forced the three of them out of the car."

Casper sat up straight. His face turned slightly gray.

Coffin Ed waited for him to comment, but he still said nothing.

"The phony cops forced him and his girl into the Buick, sapped Baron, took the six thousand, five hundred dollars and went away in the Cadillac.

"We've been all night running down the Buick. We got it and Roman. We got a statement from Roman. He claims that Baron confessed that the old woman got up after he had hit her. So it must have been the bandits in the Buick who hit her the second time and killed her."

Casper looked sick. "That's horrible," he said.

"More than you think," Grave Digger lisped.

"But I don't see what that has got to do with the robbery."

"I'm coming to that," Coffin Ed said.

Casper couldn't see Coffin Ed's face distinctly in the shadows, and it worried him. "Come over here and sit down where I can hear you," he said.

"I'll talk louder," Coffin Ed said.

A flicker of anger passed over Casper's face, but he said nothing. He picked up the gold lighter, and relit his cigar and hid behind a cloud of smoke.

"So far we haven't got a line on Baron," Coffin Ed went on. "We checked the building superintendent where the office is located and found that it is unoccupied and for rent. The super was out last night from nine o'clock until after two.

"The Cadillac hasn't been found; there's none reported stolen.

The dealers are closed on Sundays, but there's been no report that any have been broken into.

"We found the owner of the Buick—the manager of a hardware store in Yonkers. He parked his car in front of his house when he went home at seven o'clock last night and didn't miss it until this morning. But that doesn't help us any.

"We checked the listing of notary publics in Manhattan County. There was none named Bernard Kaufman; the address was bogus and the seal was counterfeit."

"That's well and good," Casper rasped impatiently. "But where's the tie-in?"

"The bandits who robbed you deliberately ran down the old lady a few minutes later and killed her."

"Just proves they're brutal mother-rapers," Casper said, lapsing back to the Harlem vernacular of his youth. "But that's all."

"Not quite all," Grave Digger lisped.

"The old lady was not an old lady," Coffin Ed said. "He was a sort of a pansy pimp who went by the name Black Beauty."

Casper strangled on cigar smoke. Grave Digger stepped beside the bed and beat him on the back. The nurse entered at that moment and looked horrified.

"It's all right," Casper gasped. "I just strangled."

"I'll get you a glass of water and a sedative," she said, looking at Grave Digger disapprovingly. "You shouldn't talk so much, and you're not allowed to smoke, either. And beating a patient on the back," she said to Grave Digger, "is no cure for strangulation."

"It works," Grave Digger lisped.

"For chrissake, don't bother me now," Casper said roughly, wiping the tears from his cheeks with the back of his hand. "I'm busy as all hell."

The nurse left in a huff.

"All right, goddammit, he was a mother-raping pansy called Black Beauty," Casper said to Coffin Ed. "So what?"

"His straight moniker is Junior Ball," Coffin Ed replied. "This morning at nine-thirty o'clock your wife, Missus Holmes, appeared at the morgue and identified the body and has requested it be released to her for burial."

Casper gave no sign of outrage or surprise or any of the other emotions they might have expected. He began looking gutter-mean. He spat out shreds of wet tobacco and said in a hard, street-fighter's voice, "So what! If his name was Junior Ball, he was her cousin."

"What we want to know is, why would a trio of bandits who had just robbed you of fifty grand run down your wife's cousin and kill him?" Coffin Ed said.

"How in the mother-raping hell would I know?" Casper said. "And if you think she knows then ask her."

"We're going to ask her all right," Grave Digger lisped.

"Then go, goddammit, and do it!" he shouted, his face turning a vivid apoplectic shade of bright purple-black. "And don't get so mother-raping cute. I'll have you out dredging the Gowanus Canal."

"Don't lose your temper, boss—at your age you might have a stroke," Grave Digger lisped.

Casper harnessed his rage with an effort. His breath came out in a long, hard sigh. He threw the partly smoked cigar on the floor and picked up another one without looking. His hands trembled as he lit it.

"All right, boys, let's cut out the crap," he said in a conciliatory voice. "You know what I mean. I don't want my wife's name mixed up in a scandal."

"That's what we figured," Coffin Ed said.

"And don't forget I got you boys your jobs," he stated.

"Yeah, you and our army records—" Grave Digger began.

"Not to mention our marks of eighty-five and eighty-seven percent in our civil service examinations," Coffin Ed supplemented.

Casper took the cigar from his teeth and said, "All right, all right, so you think you can't be hurt." He spread his hands. "I don't want to hurt you. All I want is those mother-raping bandits caught with the minimum of publicity." He sucked smoke into his lungs and let it dribble from his wide, flat nostrils. "And you wouldn't suffer any if these mother-rapers turned up dead." He gave them a half-lidded conniving look.

"That's the way we got it figured, boss," Coffin Ed said.

"What the hell do you mean by that?" Casper flared again.

"Nothing, boss. Just that dead men don't talk, is all," Coffin Ed said.

Casper didn't move. He stared from one to the other through obsidian eyes. "If you're insinuating what I think, I'll break you both," he threatened in a voice that sounded very dangerous.

For a moment there was only the sound of labored breathing in the room. The sound of muted footsteps came from the corridor. Down on a nearby street some halfwit was racing a motor.

Finally Grave Digger said lispingly, "Don't go off half-cocked, Casper. We've all known each other too long. We just figured you wouldn't want any talk from anybody with the campaign coming up you've got to organize before November."

Casper gave in. "All right, then. But just don't try to needle me, because I don't needle. Now I'll tell you what I know, and, if that don't satisfy you, you can ask me questions.

"First, I didn't recognize any of the mother-raping bandits, and I know goddam near everybody in Harlem, either by name or by face. There ain't nobody in this town who could pull a caper like that I wouldn't know, and that about goes for you, too."

Grave Digger nodded.

"So I figure they're from out of town. Got to be. Now how would they know I was getting a fifty-G payoff? That's the fifty-thousand-dollar question. First of all, I haven't told nobody, none of my associates, my wife, nobody. Secondly, I didn't know exactly when I was going to get it myself. I knew I was getting it sometime, but I didn't know when until the committee secretary, Grover Leighton, came into my office last night and plunked it down on my desk."

"Rather early for it, wasn't it? Early in the year, I mean," Coffin Ed said.

"Yeah. I didn't expect it until April or May. That would be sooner than usual. It don't generally come through until June. But they wanted to get an early start this year. It's going to be a rough election, with all these television deals and war issues and the race problem and such crap. So how they got to know about it before I knew about it myself—I mean the exact time of the delivery—is something I can't figure."

"Maybe the secretary let it slip," Grave Digger suggested.

"Yeah. Maybe frogs are eating snakes this season," Casper conceded. "I wouldn't know. But don't you boys tackle him. Let him work it out with the other white folks"—he winked—"the Pinkertons and the commissioners and the inspectors. Me—I don't give a goddam how they found out. You boys know me—I'm a realist. I don't want no out-of-town mother-rapers robbing me. I want 'em caught—you get the idea. And if you kill 'em that's fine. You understand. I want everybody to know—everybody on this goddam green earth—that can't no mother-rapers rob Casper Holmes in Harlem and get away with it."

"We got you, boss," Coffin Ed said. "But we don't have any leads. You know everything forward and backward, we thought maybe you might have some ideas. That's why we got here ahead of the confederates."

Casper allowed himself a grim smile. Then it vanished. "What's wrong with your stool pigeons?" he asked. "They got the word around in Harlem that can't nobody have the runs without your stool pigeons telling you about it."

"We'll get to them," Grave Digger lisped.

"Well, get to them, then," Casper said. "Get to the whorehouses and the gambling joints and the dope pushers and the call girls. Goddam! Two hoods with fifty G's are going to splurge on some vice or other."

"If they're still in town," Coffin Ed said.

"If they're still in town!" Casper echoed. "Two of 'em are niggers, and the white boy's a cracker. Where the hell they going to go? Where would you go if you pulled a caper for fifty G's? Where else would you look for kicks? Harlem's the greatest town on earth. You think they're going to leave it?"

Both detectives subdued the impulse to exchange looks.

Coffin Ed said dispassionately, "Don't think we're not on it, Casper. We've been on it from the moment it jumped. People got hurt, and some got killed. You'll read about it in the newspapers. But that's neither here nor there. We took our lumps, but we ain't got thrown."

Casper looked at Grave Digger's swollen mouth. "It's a job," he said.

14

The apartment was on the fifth and top floor of an old stone-fronted building on 110th Street, overlooking the lagoon in upper Central Park.

Colored boys and girls in ski ensembles and ballet skirts were skating the light fantastic at two o'clock when Grave Digger and Coffin Ed parked their half-wrecked car before the building.

The detectives paused for a moment to watch them.

"Reminds me of Gorki," Grave Digger lisped.

"The writer or the pawnbroker?" Coffin Ed asked.

"The writer, Maxim. In his book called *Bystander.* A boy breaks through the ice and disappears. Folks rush to save him but can't find him—can't find any trace of him. He's disappeared beneath the ice. So some joker asks, 'Was there really a boy?' "

Coffin Ed looked solemn. "So he thought the hole in the ice was an act of God?"

"Must have."

"Like our friend Baron, eh?"

They went silently up the old marble steps and pushed open the old, exquisitely carved wooden doors with cut-glass panels.

"The rich used to live here," Coffin Ed remarked.

"Still do," Grave Digger said. "Just changed color. Colored rich folks always live in the places abandoned by white rich folks."

They walked through a narrow, oak-paneled hallway with stained-glass wall lamps to an old rickety elevator.

A very old colored man with long, kinky gray hair and parchment-like skin, wearing a mixed livery of some ancient, faded sort, rose slowly from a padded stool and asked courteously, "What floor, gentlemens?"

"Top," Coffin Ed said.

The old man drew his cotton-gloved hand back from the lever as though it had suddenly turned red hot.

"Mister Holmes ain't in," he said.

"Missus Holmes is," Coffin Ed said. "We have an appointment."

The old man shook his cotton-boll head. "She didn't tell me about it," he said.

"She doesn't tell you everything she does, grandfather," Coffin Ed said.

Grave Digger drew a soft leather folder from his inside pocket and lashed his shield. "We're the men," he lisped.

Stubbornly the old man shook his head. "Makes no difference to Mister Holmes. He's *The Man*."

"All right," Coffin Ed compromised. "You take us up. If Missus Holmes doesn't receive us, you bring us down. Okay?"

"It's a gentleman's agreement," the old man said.

Grave Digger belched as the ancient elevator creaked upward.

"That lets us out," Coffin Ed said. "Gentlemen don't belch."

"Gentlemen don't eat pig ears and collard greens," Grave Digger said. "They don't know what they're missing."

The old man gave the appearance of not hearing.

Casper had the whole top floor to himself. It had originally been built for two families with facing doors across a small elevator foyer, but one had been closed and plastered over and there was only the one red-lacquered one left, with a small, engraved brass nameplate in the middle of the upper panel, announcing: *Casper Holmes.*

"Might just as well say Jesus Christ," Grave Digger said.

"Go light on this lady, Digger," Coffin Ed cautioned as he pushed the bell buzzer.

"Don't I always?" Grave Digger said.

A young black man in a spotless white jacket opened the door. It opened so silently Grave Digger blinked. The young man had shining black curls that looked as though they had been milled from coal tar, a velvet-smooth forehead slightly greasy, and dark-brown eyes, with whites like muddy water, devoid of all intelligence. His flat nose lay against low, narrow cheeks slashed by a thin-lipped mouth of tremendous width. The mouth was filled with white, even teeth.

"Mister Jones and Mister Johnson?" he inquired.

"As if you didn't know," Grave Digger said.

"Please come right this way, sirs," he said, leading them to a front room off the front of the hall.

He came as far as the doorway and left them.

It was a big room with windows overlooking Central Park. In the distance, over treetops, the towers of Rockefeller Center and the Empire Sate Building loomed in the murky haze. It reminded Ed of the lounge of the City Club.

Grave Digger lifted his feet high to keep from stumbling over the thick nap of the Oriental rugs, and Coffin Ed eyed the ornate furniture warily, wondering where he should sit.

Jazz classics were stacked on a combination set, and at their entrance Louis Armstrong was doing an oldy called *Where The Chickens Don't Roost So High.*

"Me and my old lady used to dance to that tune at the Savoy—before they tore it down," Grave Digger said, and started cutting the rug.

He still had on his hat and overcoat, and he was performing the intricate steps of an old-time jitterbug with great abandon. His swollen lips were pecking at the perfumed air, and his overcoat tails were flapping in the breeze.

Coffin Ed stood beside a Louis XIV love seat, scratching his ribs.

"Digger, you're a pappy," he said. "Those steps you're doing went out with zoot suits."

"Don't I know it," Grave Digger said, sighing.

Mrs. Holmes swung into the room from an inner doorway like a stripteaser coming on stage. She stopped short in open-mouth amazement and put her hands on her hips.

"If you want to dance, go to the Theresa ballroom," she said in a cool contralto voice. "There's a matinee this afternoon."

Grave Digger froze with a foot in the air, and Coffin Ed laughed: "Haw haw."

In unison they turned and stared at Mrs. Holmes.

She had the type of beauty made fashionable in the 1930's by an all-colored musical called *Brownskin Models.* She was rather short and busty, with a pear-shaped bottom and slender legs. She had short wavy hair, a heart-shaped face, and long-lashed, expressive brown eyes; and her mouth was like a red carnation.

She wore gold lamé slacks, which fitted so tight that every quiver of a muscle showed. Her waist was drawn in by a black leather belt, four inches wide, decorated with gilt figures. Her breasts stuck out from a turtleneck blue jersey-silk pullover as though taking dead aim at any man in front of her. Black, gilt-edged Turkish slippers turned up at the toes made her feet seem too small to support her. The combination of gold fingernail polish, sparkling rings, and dangling charm bracelets gave her hands the appearance of jewelry-store windows.

Both men whipped off their hats and stood there, looking gawky and sheepish.

"I was just relaxing a bit," Grave Digger lisped. "We've had a hard night."

She glanced at his swollen lips and broke out a slow, insinuating smile. "You shouldn't love so strenuously," she murmured.

Grave Digger felt the heat spread over his face. Coffin Ed seemed to be having trouble figuring what to do with his feet.

She walked toward a pair of divans flanking an imitation fireplace on the far side of the room. Her hips rolled with the slow tantalizing motion of a natural-born teaser. Grave Digger was thinking how he could put his hands about her waist, while Coffin Ed was telling himself that she was the type of female who would set a man on fire and then direct him to a river.

Electric logs gave off a red glow. She sat down with her back to the windows and tucked a leg beneath her. She knew the red light on the colors of her skin and ensemble made her look exotic. Her eyes became luminous.

She waved them to a seat on the facing divan. Between them there was a huge circular table about knee-high, made by cutting down a dining room table. It was littered with the Sunday papers. Casper's face peered out from beneath the headlines about the robbery.

"You want to talk to me about my cousin," she said.

"Well, it's like this," Coffin Ed said. "We're trying to find the connection between Black Beauty and a man named Baron."

She frowned prettily. "It doesn't make any sense to me. I don't know anyone named Black Beauty or Baron."

The detectives stared at her for a moment. Grave Digger leaned forward and placed his hat atop the newspapers. Neither of them had removed their overcoats.

"Black Beauty's your cousin," Grave Digger lisped.

"Oh," she said. "I've never heard him called by that name. Who told you that?"

"It's in the newspapers," Coffin Ed said.

Her eyes widened. "Really." She shifted slightly so that the red light shone on her black belt with its tracery of gilded designs. "I didn't pay any attention. I was so upset." She shuddered and covered her face with her hands. Her breasts trembled. Looking at them, Grave Digger wondered how she did it.

"I understand," Coffin Ed said sympathetically. "What I don't understand is how did you know he was your cousin, Junior Ball, since all the papers referred to him as Black Beauty."

She took her hands from her face and stared at him haughtily. "Are you cross-examining me?" she asked in a cold, imperious voice.

"More or less," Grave Digger lisped, his voice getting dry.

She jumped to her feet. "Then you may leave," she said.

Coffin Ed gave Grave Digger an accusing look, then looked up at Mrs. Holmes and spread his hands entreatingly.

"Listen, Missus Holmes, we've had a long hard night. We're just trying to catch the bandits who robbed your husband. We know you want them caught as much as he does. We're not trying to antagonize you. That's the last thing we want to do. We're just following a thin lead. Won't you bear with us for a few minutes?"

She looked from him to Grave Digger. He looked back at her as though he would like to whip her.

But he said in a thick, dry lisp, "I didn't mean it the way you took it. My nerves are kind of raw."

"So are mine," she said in a voice that had roughened.

She kept staring into Grave Digger's hot, rapacious gaze until her body seemed to melt; and she sat down again as though from lack of strength.

"But if you are civil I will help you all I can," she relented.

Coffin Ed was fumbling about in his mind for a way to phrase his questions. "Well, the thing is," he said, "we'd like to know what Ball did—his occupation."

"He was a dress designer," she said. "And he made articles from leather."

She noticed Grave Digger staring at her belt and squirmed slightly.

"Did he make your belt?" he asked.

She hesitated as though she might refuse to answer, then reluctantly said, "Yes."

Grave Digger had made out some of the gilded designs encircling the belt. They depicted a series of Pans with nude males and females caught in grotesque postures on their horns. The thought struck him suddenly that Junior Ball got gored by one of his own Pans.

Coffin Ed picked up the idea. "Did he ever work for Baron?" he asked. "Design anything for him?"

"I've told you I don't know this Baron," she said, her voice still rough. "What has he got to do with all of this?"

"Well, I'll tell you how it goes," he said, and related the statement they had got from Roman. "So you see how it figures," he concluded. "Your cousin, Ball, and this man, Baron, were in some kind of racket."

She frowned, but this time not prettily. "It is possible," she conceded. "Although I can't see why Junior should have been mixed up in any kind of racket. He was doing well in his own field; he didn't need anything. And I still don't understand how this man, Baron, can help you find the scum who robbed Casper."

"He got a good look at them, for one thing," Coffin Ed said. "He talked to them; he knows their voices."

"And we have a hunch he knew them from before," Grave Digger added.

She sighed theatrically. "I've gotten used to a lot of strange things with my husband in politics," she said. "But all this terrible, horrible violence is too much for me." A tremor ran over her body, making all of it shake.

Grave Digger licked his swollen lips. He was thinking about some of the lonely women about town he hadn't stopped in to see lately.

She knew what he was thinking and gave him a quick up-from-under look, her big brown eyes stark naked for an instant; then she turned her face away and looked into the fire, and her expression became sad.

"I'd better not catch him on a dark street," Grave Digger lisped in a voice so thick it was blurred.

She whirled about and stared at him. "Oh!" The red light on her face seemed to be reflected from somewhere underneath the brown of her skin. "I thought you said—" She thought he'd said, *"I'd better not catch you on a dark street."* She was flustered for a moment. It made her furious with herself.

"I've helped you all I can," she said abruptly. She began trembling in earnest. "Please go. I can't stand any more of this." Her eyes brimmed with tears. She looked even more desirable than with her brassy manner.

Coffin Ed stood up and tapped Grave Digger on the shoulder. Grave Digger came out of his trance with a start.

"Just one more thing," Coffin Ed said. "Do you know if Junior saw your husband last night?"

"I don't know. Don't ask me anything else," she said tearfully. "All I know is what I've read in the newspapers. I haven't talked to Casper. He's still in a coma. And I don't know—" She stopped as though struck by a sudden thought, then said, "And if you're so interested in Junior's business, go down on Nineteenth Street and talk to his associate, Zog Ziegler. He ought to know."

For an instant the two detectives were held in an imperceptible rigidity, as though listening for a sound to be repeated that had come from far away.

"Zog Ziegler," Coffin Ed repeated in a flat voice. "Do you know his address."

"Somewhere on East Nineteenth Street," she said. "Just go down and look. You'll know the house when you see it."

She sounded hysterically anxious for them to leave.

"Good day, Missus Holmes, and thank you," Coffin Ed said, and Grave Digger said, "You've helped us more than you know."

She stiffened slightly at the subtle jibe in his words, but she didn't look up.

The wide-mouthed boy in the white jacket appeared in the doorway as though by magic. He let them out.

After an interminable delay, the creaking elevator made its appearance. The old elevator operator with the cotton-boll head refused to look at them for reasons of his own. They left him to his solitude.

When they came out into the street, big fat snowflakes were drifting from a solid gray sky. The motionless air had become degrees warmer, and the snowflakes stack where they landed, too heavy to roll over.

"She knew what I meant, the teasing bitch."

"Didn't we all."

"She never did answer your question."

"She said enough."

They stood looking at their wreck of a car for a moment before getting in.

"We'd better change buggies before going downtown," Grave Digger said. "We might get booked on vag."

"We can go back to the station and get my car."

"We might stop at Fats's for a couple of shots."

"Whisky ain't going to help us think any better," Coffin Ed cautioned.

"Hell, beat as I am now it don't matter," Grave Digger said.

15

It was four o'clock when Casper got finished with the brass and the half-brass. He had had it with the chief inspector, the inspector in charge of the Homicide squads, Lieutenant Brogan and a detective stenographer from Homicide, and two lieutenants from the Central Office Bureaus.

They had handled him gently, with all due respect for the tender sensibilities of a vote-getting politician, but he had been through the wringer nevertheless.

What they had hammered on mainly was the mystery of the leak. One or the other kept pointing out that the hoods got the tip-off from somewhere, that it didn't come from heaven, until Casper blew his top.

"I tipped them!" he had exploded. "I leaked it. I said come on and get it. Knock out my mother-raping brains and kill a couple of people. Is that what you think?"

"It could have been somebody in your organization," the chief inspector had said.

"All right, it was somebody in my organization. Then go out and arrest them. All of 'em! Start with my two secretaries. Haul in my associates. Don't forget my field workers. Not to mention my wife. Take 'em all downtown. Give 'em the third degree. Tickle 'em with your mother-raping loaded hose. And see what you get. You'll get nuttin', because they didn't know nuttin'. At least if they did, they didn't get it from me, because I didn't know the payoff was coming through when it did my own damn self."

No one had batted an eye at the outburst.

"Grover Leighton said he told you several days ago that he'd bring it up Saturday night," the chief inspector had said quietly. "He doesn't remember the exact day."

"He doesn't remember because he didn't do it," Casper had raved.

"Maybe he thinks he did. But Grover has the whole fifty states to think of; and if you think he can remember every goddam little thing he has done you're giving him credit for having a mechanical brain."

They had let it go at that.

Now Casper had a headache the likes of which would have made his professed coma preferable.

A colored trainee nurse had come in to straighten up and remove the saucers filled with cigar butts. She had opened the French windows to clear the air, and the sight of the heavy fall of snow added to Casper's fury.

"Now they'll send in Canadian truckers," he muttered.

The little girl glanced at him apprehensively; she didn't know whether she was supposed to answer or not. She began edging toward the door.

The telephone on the night stand rang. He snatched up the receiver and shouted, "Tell 'em I'm dead!"

The cool, controlled voice of the reception nurse asked, "Do you care to see the press? Our lobby down here is packed with reporters and photographers."

"Tell 'em I'm still in a coma."

"They've seen the police leave."

"Then tell 'em to go to hell. Tell 'em I've had a relapse. Tell 'em I've developed brain fever. No, don't tell 'em that. Tell them I'm resting now and that I'll see them at eight o'clock."

"Yes, sir. And there is a telephone call for you from the Pinkerton Detective Agency. Shall I put it through?"

He hesitated for an instant, waiting for his sixth sense to work; but it lay dead.

"All right, I'll take it," he said.

A calm, soothing-type voice said, "Mister Casper Holmes?"

"Speaking," Casper said.

"I am Herbert Peters from the Pinkerton Detective Agency. Mister Grover Leighton has been in contact with us, and he has engaged us to arrange for an ambulance under guard to transport you from the hospital to your home."

"Why not a baby carriage?" Casper growled.

Peters chuckled faintly. "If you will give us the approximate time you will be checking out, we'll make all the necessary arrangements."

"I'll arrange for my own transportation when I leave," Casper said. "But I'm not thinking of leaving for two or three days."

"Then you think you will be checking out on Tuesday?"

"That's what I think. But I don't think I need any of you. If I can't get from here to my own house, I need to go back to the nursery."

"That's not exactly the situation, sir," Peters said. "It is not a matter of your ability to take care of yourself. One of our men has been killed, and, unfortunately, you are a witness to the murder. As long as you are alive, the murderers are in danger of—"

"You ain't just saying it," Casper cut in.

"So Mister Leighton feels it is essential that we give you the protection necessary for a public figure whose life is in danger."

"Mister Leighton has already made one mistake by going ahead on his own," Casper said.

"That's why he doesn't want to make another," Peters said. "That's why we are requesting your co-operation in advance." He paused for a moment, then added, "We will have to cover you in any event, whether you like it or not; but it would be much better all around if we had your co-operation."

Casper conceded. "All right. I'll call you tomorrow and tell you when I'm checking out. Will you be there?"

"If I'm not, someone else will."

"Okay, give me the number."

When he had hung up, he waited for a minute, then dialed the number he'd been given.

An unfamiliar voice said, "Pinkerton Detective Agency."

"Let me speak to Herbert Peters."

"Who's calling, please."

"Casper Holmes."

A moment later Peters' calm voice said, "Yes, Mister Holmes?"

"I'm just checking," Casper said. "Being as I can't look through the telephone and see just who really is phoning me."

"I understand, Mister Holmes. Is that all, sir?"

"That's all."

Casper cradled the receiver and sat up in bed, thinking. The trainee had finished and closed the windows and left, but he hadn't noticed.

He lifted the receiver and told the switchboard operator not to put through any more calls.

"If someone telephones, what shall I say?"

"Say that I am sleeping and ask them to phone back after eight o'clock."

"Yes, sir."

"And give me an outside line."

When he heard the central office buzz, he dialed a number.

A woman's voice answered. "Hel-looo?"

"Marie?"

"Yes. Is that you, Casper?"

"Yeah. Is Joe in?"

"Yes. I'll call him. How's your noggin?"

"Palpitating. Let me talk to Joe."

He heard her calling, "Jooooe! It's Casper."

Joe Green was the biggest numbers banker in Harlem; he had a part of three lotteries.

"Casper, how's the boy?" he greeted in a husky voice.

"Ain't nothing that a little sleep won't cure."

"Can't hurt you hitting you on the head," Joe said. "But snatching all that long green off you must have given you a running fit."

"It wasn't mine," Casper said. "They didn't hurt nothing but my feelings."

"And you'll never forgive the mother-rapers for that."

"Now that's for sure. But what I called you for is I want to borrow a couple of your boys for later in the day."

"For bodyguards or running errands?"

"I'm going to check out here at seven-thirty in one of Clay's hearses—"

Joe chuckled. "Just don't go by the way of the cemetery, daddy."

Casper laughed. "By way of Clay, neither. Naw, I'm going home. I want to dodge the newsboys; I got a pop call to make on the way. I just want them to trail me."

"It's done," Joe said. "How 'bout Big Six and George Drake in the Cadillac? They ought to handle any situation that might jump up. Or do you want another one?"

"Naw, they'll do. I want them to pick up the hearse at Clay's and stay with it, but not too close. I don't want it looking like no procession."

"I got you, daddy. What time?"

"I'm leaving here at seven-thirty. They'd better get to Clay's by seven."

Joe hesitated. "Can't you make it earlier, daddy? If this snow keeps coming down like it is now, ain't much going to be moving by seven-thirty."

"I'm going to be moving," Casper said.

"Okay, daddy, I got you covered," Joe said. "Don't do nothing I wouldn't do."

"It's made, then," Casper said. "I'll see you in church."

When the connection was broken, he began dialing another number without putting down the receiver.

A proper male voice said, "H. Exodus Clay's Funeral Parlor. Good afternoon. May we be of service to you?"

"I don't want to be buried, if that's what you mean," Casper said. "Just let me speak to Clay."

"Mr. Clay is resting; he's having his customary afternoon nap. Perhaps I can help you."

"Wake him up," Casper said. "This is Casper Holmes."

"Oh, Mister Holmes. Yes, sir, right away, sir."

A few moments later Clay's thin, querulous voice came over the wire. "Casper. I was hoping to do some business with you."

"You are, Hank, but not the kind you want." Only a few people in Harlem knew that the H in Clay's name stood for Henry; most people thought it stood for either Heaven or Hell. "I want to hire a hearse."

"For yourself, or for a friend?"

"For myself."

"The reason I asked, I have three hearses now. I use the old one for poor folks, the middle one for rich, and the new one for celebrities. I'll give you the new one."

"Naw, give me the middle-newest. I don't want to attract any attention to myself. I want to slip away from this hospital without anybody seeing me. And let Jackson drive it; nobody going to look at him twice."

"Jackson!" Clay echoed. "Listen, Casper, I don't want any shenanigans with my hearse. I never will forget the time Jackson was running all over town dodging the police with my hearse full of dead bodies."

"What are you beefing about?" Casper said. "He made you a lot of business."

"I'd rather get my business in the normal way; I'm not expecting a depression."

"All right, Hank, have it your way. I just want to get this hearse over here at the back door at seven-thirty sharp."

"The streets will be snowed under by that time," Clay complained. "Can't you make it earlier, or wait another day?"

"Naw. Just put some chains on it. And there's going to be

some boys of Joe Green's following it. So don't let that worry you."

"Boys of Joe Green's!" Clay exclaimed apprehensively. "Listen, Casper, if anything happens to my hearse, I'm going to bill the national party for it."

"Okay, you do that. And tell Jackson to drive me first to my office on One-twenty-fifth Street."

"Tell him yourself," Clay said, losing interest and already drifting back to sleep.

Casper cradled the receiver and picked up his wrist watch from the night stand. It was thirteen minutes past five o'clock. He peered between the drawn curtains at the drifting snow. Everything that met his eye was white, except the gray sky. He selected a cigar, clipped it carefully, stuck one end between his lips and rolled it about. Then, he put it down on the edge of the night stand, picked up the receiver again and began dialing.

"Do you want an outside line?" the operator asked.

"What the hell do you think I'm dialing for," he said.

He waited for the dial tone and began over. He heard the phone ringing at the other end.

A cool, contralto voice said, "Yes."

"Leila. Casper," he said.

"How are you, sugar," she said in the same tone that she had said yes.

"Listen, I'll be home around eight o'clock," he said. His voice was as impersonal as hers. "I want you to stay there until after I get there—or say until nine o'clock. Then you can go wherever in the hell you want to. Understand?"

"I'm not deaf."

"Naw, but you're dumb sometimes."

"That blow on your head hasn't changed your disposition," she observed.

"If anybody phones me, tell them I'm still in the hospital and won't be home until Tuesday. Tell them I've had a relapse and am in a coma again. Get that?"

"Yes, sugar, I got it." Under her breath she added, "And I'm going to keep it, too."

"What's that?"

"I didn't say anything. Somebody must be talking on your end."

"All right. And for once keep your lip buttoned up."

"Is that all?"

He put down the receiver and reached for his cigar. Before he could pick it up, the phone rang. He picked up the receiver again.

"What is it?"

"Washington, D.C., calling," the operator said. "A Mister Grover Leighton. Shall I put him through?"

"Yes."

Grover's sunshiny, glad-handing Pennsylvania voice came on. "Casper. How are you?"

"Fine. Just resting. It's all I can do at the moment."

"That's the thing to do. Just keep it up. We've all been worried about you."

"Nothing to worry about. You can't hurt an old dog like me." Casper's voice had taken on a subtle obsequious quality.

"That's what I told them," Grover said cheerfully. "And don't you worry, either. We'll come through again soon with the same score."

"Oh, I'm not worrying about that," Casper said. "But some of the city brass here have been making it a little rough."

"For you?" Grover sounded slightly shocked. "Why so?"

"They're trying to figure out how the hoods got the tip-off," Casper said. "And the chief inspector claims that you told him that you had told me sometime early last week that you were stopping by last night with the payroll."

There was a pause as though Grover was trying to remember. "Well, I guess I did tell him something like that," he said finally. "But I thought I told you about it Wednesday, or was it Thursday, when we talked on the phone about the precinct units."

"Listen, Grover, I want you to think, try to remember. Because I'm sure you didn't tell me then. You might forget a thing like that, but I wouldn't. All I've got to think of is my little group in Harlem, while you've got the whole country on your mind. And I'm sure I wouldn't have forgotten your telling me that, because that's what starts the cart to rolling."

"Maybe you're right," Grover conceded. "It was in my mind to tell you, but it must have slipped. But that's not important, is it?"

"Not to you and me; but the brass here are insinuating that the leak came from me."

"My God!" Grover sounded really shocked. "They must be *crazy*. They're not trying to push you around, are they?"

"Naw, it's not that. But I don't like all the innuendo, especially at the beginning of a campaign."

"You're right. I'll telephone the chief inspector and put an end to that. And when they're arrested we'll find out where they got their information. But I telephoned you about another matter. I have asked the Pinkerton Agency in New York to keep an eye on you; we don't want a duplication of this business, and we certainly don't want anything to happen to you. And they are involved now also, since they lost one of their men."

"You know I'll co-operate, Grover. Be glad to. It's as much to my interest as to anyone's."

"That's what I told them. I asked them to arrange for an ambulance with a guard to take you home when you leave there—unless, of course, you have arranged something else."

"Naw, I haven't made any arrangements," Casper said. "That suits me fine. One of the men phoned from the agency, said you had spoken to them. I told him I'd let him know in advance when I planned to leave."

"Well, then, it's all settled." Grover sounded relieved. "Take care of yourself, Casper. We don't want anything to happen to you. The Harlem vote is going to be mighty important in this coming election. It might mean the balance that will swing the whole state of New York in our favor."

"I'm going to take damn good care of myself from now on," Casper said.

Grover laughed. "Good fellow! Let us know if there is anything we can do for you."

"Nothing at the moment, Grover. Thanks for everything."

"Don't mention it. We'll be thanking you before it's done with."

When they had hung up, Casper lit his cigar and sat smoking it slowly, looking thoughtful.

"It's in the fire now," he said to no one, and picked up the receiver again.

"Give me a line, honey," he said.

He dialed a downtown number.

"Now who can this be?" a voice of indeterminate gender asked with an affected lisp.

"Let me speak to Johnny."

"Oh, and not with me?"

Casper didn't answer.

"And who shall I tell him is calling, dear?"

"None of your God-damned business."

"Oh! You're rude!"

He heard the receiver dropped on a table-top. After what seemed to him much longer than was necessary, a pleasant male tenor voice said, "Hello, Casper, it couldn't be anybody but you who'd be so unkind to Zog."

"I'm going home around eight o'clock," Casper said. "I want you to come up later."

"I knew they couldn't hurt you," Johnny said, and then, "How much later?"

"Around ten o'clock. Use your own key and come on in."

"Will do," Johnny said.

When Johnny had hung up, Casper jiggled the hook and asked the operator to have the supervising nurse come up to his room.

16

It was past four o'clock when Grave Digger and Coffin Ed got away from Fats's Down Home Restaurant—just about the time Casper had got finished with the brass.

They hadn't intended to stay that long. But the place was filled with gamblers and whorehouse madams, all curious about the Casper caper, and they had been fishing themselves, to see what they could pick up about any new jokers in town on a kick binge.

The gamblers hadn't run across any fresh money; if they had, they wouldn't admit it. The madams hadn't come across any mew customers, not with big money, anyway.

"If I had," one madam confessed, "I'd have handcuffed each of 'em to two girls, and foot-chained 'em to the bed, bad as I need money."

Pee Wee, the giant black bartender, had fixed them some hot bourbon teas to stave off grippe and pneumonia. Before they had a chance to test what those potent drinks might stave off, they were clutched in the throes of tremendous appetites.

Then Fats had appeared, looking like the scalded and scraped carcass of a hippopotamus, and said he was taking a Smithfield ham out of the oven. That did it.

They ate baked ham and sweet potatoes while Grave Digger held everybody entranced giving a detailed account of the joker getting his head cut off.

By the time they got back outside, they were both willing to believe the gremlins had done it.

The snow was drifting down like endless fields of cotton, and the street was covered an inch thick. Their wreck of a car, sitting at the curb, looked like an abandoned derelict. They hadn't got to the precinct station as yet.

Grave Digger took hold of Coffin Ed's sleeve and detained him for a discussion on criminology.

"Take a detective," he said. "Like you and me. A man gets robbed in the street. The robber taps his victim on the head, knocks him unconscious and runs. Ain't nobody seen him; the victim don't know him. Then we come up. We don't know a damn thing. Don't even know the man's been robbed. All we got is his word for it. But everybody expects us to run off and nab the criminals as if we got a robber's preserve."

"Maybe they expect us to crawl along and sniff them out, like human bloodhounds," Coffin Ed said. "Maybe they think we got the nose for it."

"That Casper," Grave Digger said. "He got more twists in him than a barrel full of snakes."

They got into the car. Normally at that hour it would have been dark, but the blanket of snow seemed to illuminate the streets. The few cars out were crawling along like snails, leaving black lines on the white blanket.

"Two bull alligators like you and me ain't going to catch anything in that goldfish bowl downtown," Coffin Ed stated. "We're just going to scare the living hell out of everybody and get the deep freeze for our effort."

"We'll bait the hook," Grave Digger suggested.

"I was thinking the same thing."

Captain Rice was on duty in the precinct station. They asked his permission to take the prisoner along to identify Baron in case they unearthed him. The captain said a Homicide detective had taken Roman Hill down to the Bureau of Criminal Identification at Headquarters, but he gave them an order to pick him up. He was still a precinct prisoner until he appeared before the magistrate's court the next morning. They changed over to Coffin Ed's new Plymouth and went down the East Side Drive. Coffin Ed took the wheel; he didn't mind riding with Grave Digger in a city-owned car, but he had paid his own money for the Plymouth.

The small tractor-type snowplows were already at work on the main arteries, scurrying about like orange bugs, piling the snow along the curbs for the trucks to pick up and dump into the river.

The tires sang in the coating of snow, and the windshield wipers clicked back and forth.

They talked about the blizzard of 1949, when city traffic had been paralyzed by thirty-nine inches of snow.

Off to their left, unseen tugboats with green and red lights, barely discernible through the white curtain, raised a cacophony of foghorns. The lights of the petroleum companies across the East River were blanked out.

A ferryboat was docked at the 79th Street pier when they passed, unloading day workers from Welfare Island.

"Damn, this day is moving," Grave Digger remarked.

They began feeling the pressure of time. A slow buildup of apprehension sobered them.

Coffin Ed stepped on the gas.

They found Roman in the Gallery on the first floor of Headquarters on Centre Street.

Headquarters, and the Annex across the street, were the only lighted buildings in the area. Skyscrapers in the adjacent Wall Street district loomed dark and ghostly against the bottomless gray sky.

They gave the Homicide detective Captain Rice's order and took the prisoner. He looked scarcely the worse for the headwhipping he had taken; just a mass of unnoticeable clotted wounds in his thick curly hair.

"Do you want the other one, too?" the detective asked. "The bartender from the Paris Bar?"

"You still got him?"

"Got him and going to keep him until he looks at every picture on record—unless you want him."

"You keep him," Grave Digger said. "Nothing we can do with him."

They handcuffed Roman and took him out to the Plymouth. Coffin Ed had left the motor running and the windshield wipers working. But he had to brush the snow from all the windows before he could move on.

They went a couple of blocks beyond Headquarters and stopped.

"You got a sailor suit?" Coffin Ed asked.

"Yeah, but I don't wear it," Roman said.

"Where is it?"

"It's aboard ship."

"All right, we're going over to Brooklyn to get it, and you're going to put it on," Coffin Ed said, easing the car off slowly through the snow.

When the telephone rang again, Leila Holmes thought it was Casper calling back.

"Yes." She sounded cold enough to make icicles.

"Let me talk with Casper," a man's voice said.

The hand holding the receiver began to tremble. She thought she recognized the voice, but she wasn't certain.

"He's still in the hospital," she said, a sudden indeterminable fear making her voice sound parrotlike. "He's had a relapse; he's in a coma."

"Can the bull," the voice said. "That li'l lick on a booger's head ain't putting him in no coma."

She felt certain of it now. It was a Southern voice with a Mississippi accent. It was a white man's voice.

She began trembling all over, her breasts moving in the jersey-silk pullover like molded Jell-O.

"Telephone the hospital if you don't believe me," she said, furious with herself for sounding defensive, but she couldn't help it. She was scared witless. There was something sadistic and inhuman about the voice. "He is in a coma," she contended.

"If he wants any of his fifty G's back, he better come out of it," the voice said. "And nigger-quick."

The use of the epithet steadied her fear and scalded her with rage. "Who are you, you mother-raping peckerwood," she flared.

An evil chuckle came over the wire. "I'm the man who can help him get his money back—for a split," the voice said.

She tried to think, but she didn't know where to start. "You'd better call Casper at the hospital," she said.

"You call him, sugar pie. I've called six times and can't get through to him. So you do it, honey chile."

"What shall I tell him?" she asked, then added viciously, "Red-neck."

"I'll make your li'l neck red if I get hold of you," the voice said, then added, "just tell him what I told you, and if he wants to do business, he better take my call."

She remembered what Casper had told her about keeping her lip buttoned up. If she did the wrong thing, he'd be furious. She didn't know what to do.

"It can keep, can't it?" she said.

"Keep until when?"

"Until he gets out the hospital."

"When will that be?"

"When?" She felt trapped. "I don't know when. Ask at the hospital."

"You ain't doing him no good, baby doll," the voice taunted. "He ain't going to like it when he finds out what he's missed."

"All right, sonofabitch!" she flared. "I'll call him and you call me back."

"What good is that going to do? I got to do business with him.

And it ain't going to keep. If Casper wants to lie in the hospital with his head underneath the pillow, that's just going to be his bad luck. And I'll figure out some other way to get my split."

Her mind exploded with vulgarity, as it always did when she felt cornered.

"For chrissakes, call back after eight o'clock," she said exasperatedly. "I don't know what the hell—"

She didn't get a chance to finish it. A soft click sounded from the other end, and the line went dead. She sat staring at the receiver. She began trembling again. Scare went through her like acid.

"Now what the hell did I say?" she wondered.

It was twenty minutes past six when the telephone rang.

A proper male voice answered. "H. Exodus Clay's Funeral Parlor. Good evening. May we be of service to you?"

"This is the Pinkerton Detective Agency," the voice said at the other end. "Leave me speak to the boss."

It was a Southern voice with a Mississippi accent. It was a white man's voice.

The attendant said, "Yes, sir. Right away, sir."

A moment later Clay's querulous voice came on the line, "What is it now?"

"This is the Pinkerton Detective Agency," the voice repeated.

"You said that before," Clay snapped. "This is my funeral parlor. Now let's get on."

"We are sending three men up to your place to guard the ambulance you're sending for Mister Holmes," the voice informed him.

During the past hour, the voice had repeated the same words to sixteen other ambulance services and funeral homes in Harlem without the desired result. But this time the voice struck pay dirt.

"It's not an ambulance I'm sending," Clay said tartly. "It's a hearse."

A chuckle came over the wire. "That's just the right thing," the voice said. "What time are you sending it?"

"Casper has arranged for his own guards," Clay replied with a note of racial pride in his thin, peevish voice. "We're all local people up here. We don't need any big-time race-track detectives with machine guns just to go a few blocks down the street. Inform your employers that it's already covered."

"That's mighty fine," the voice said. "But we've been employed by the national party. We'll cover the coverers."

"Well, you'd better hurry, then. It'll leave here in half an hour."

"That'll work out fine," the voice said. "We won't interfere with any of the arrangements; we'll keep in the background. You don't even have to mention us."

"You needn't worry about that," Clay said sarcastically. "I don't get paid to advertise the Pinkertons."

With that rejoinder he clapped down the receiver.

There was a traffic jam on the Brooklyn Bridge.

A trailer truck had skidded on a spot of slick ice caused by the overheated radiator of a passenger car that had passed a short time previously, and sideswiped a passenger bus.

There were no casualties, but the truck bumper had gored a hole in the side of the bus and it took time to get them apart.

Grave Digger and Coffin Ed sat in the stalled line of cars and fumed. They had the feeling that time was rushing past like a maniac with a knife and they were caught barefooted with their hands tied. They couldn't back out, couldn't squeeze through; they couldn't abandon the car on the bridge and walk.

Roman sat in the back in his sailor's suit, white cap stuck on the back of his head and his manacled hands in his lap.

Grave Digger looked at his watch. It was twenty minutes past six. The snow was coming down.

"I'd rather be bit in the rear by a boa constrictor than sitting here waiting for something to happen, and I can't even guess what," he complained bitterly.

"All I'm waiting to happen is for them to get those wrecks apart," Coffin Ed grated.

It was three minutes past seven when they turned into East 19th Street from Third Avenue and began looking for the house.

They had no trouble finding it. It had a four-story yellow brick-veneer front, with candy-striped awnings at all the upper windows sagging with snow. The first-floor lounge had a wide picture window overlooking a three-foot strip of lawn. The window curtains were a translucent pale-blue silk, behind which the silhouettes of people moved in a frantic saraband. Black steps led up to a door covered with a plate of blackened bronze set in a white frame. In the upper panel was a knocker that looked vaguely obscene; overhead was a carriage lamp.

Coffin Ed drove past and parked three houses beyond. In unison they turned about and looked at Roman.

"We want you to go in that house back there and ask for Junior Ball," Grave Digger lisped.

"I didn't understand you," Roman said.

"Let me talk," Coffin Ed said to Grave Digger.

Grave Digger waved him ahead.

Coffin Ed repeated the order.

"Yes, sir," Roman said, then asked, "What do I say to him if he's there?"

"He ain't there," Coffin Ed said. "He's dead. They know he's dead, but you're not supposed to know. You just got off shipboard and you came looking for him at this address that he gave you last time your ship was in."

"I'm supposed to be one of those?"

"That's right."

"What do I do when they tell me he's dead?"

"They're not going to tell you. They're going to invite you in and ask you to wait; they'll tell you they expect Junior to arrive any minute."

"What do I do while I'm waiting?"

"Hell, boy, where have you been all your life? It's a pansy crib. They'll find things for you to do."

"I don't go for that stuff," Roman muttered.

"What kind of square are you? This ain't the docks. These are highbrows. Who do you think you're going to find in a hundred-thousand-dollar house a block away from Gramercy Square? They're going to try to make you, but they're going to test you first. You just sit there and drink your cocktails and look embarrassed—"

"That ain't going to be hard."

"Act like you're waiting for Junior. Then, after about five minutes, start looking impatient. Let your eyes rove around. Then ask whoever you're talking to what time will Baron be in."

"Baron!" Roman sat up straight. "Mister Baron? The man who sold me my car? Is he going to be in there?"

"We don't know. He might; he might not. If you see him when you go in, you just grab him and yell for help."

"I won't need no help," Roman declared.

"Yes, you will," Coffin Ed said. "Because we don't want him hurt. You just grab him and hold on to him and start yelling."

"What if he tries to draw a pistol on me?" Roman wanted to know.

"If you hold him tight enough he'll forget it."

"I's ready if you is," Roman said.

"Okay," Coffin Ed said. "We're going to back up and park next door. When you hear me blowing on the horn one time long and twice short, you come on out."

"Yes, sir, but I sure hope to see Mister Baron before that."

"So do we, so do we," Coffin Ed said.

Grave Digger leaned over the back of the seat, unlocked the handcuffs about Roman's wrists and removed them.

"Okay, go ahead," he said. "Just remember one thing. You might run, but you can't hide."

"I ain't going to run," Roman said.

They watched him walking in his rolling sailor's gait back to the bronze door and stand looking at the knocker as though he didn't know what to do with it. They saw him knock on the door with his knuckles.

"He must have never left his ship," Coffin Ed observed.

Grave Digger grunted.

They saw the door open; a moment later they saw him go inside; they saw the door close. Coffin Ed started the motor and backed up the car.

17

A black Cadillac limousine with scarcely any metal trimmings was parked on 134th Street, a few doors down from Clay's Funeral Parlor, on the opposite side of the street. It might have been a funeral car judging from its somber appearance.

The motor was idling, but it couldn't be heard. The defroster was on, the lights were off. The windshield wipers clicked back and forth.

George Drake sat behind the wheel, cleaning his fingernails with a tiny, gold-handled penknife. He was an ordinary-looking colored man of indeterminate age. Even the expensive dark clothes he wore looked ordinary on him. His only distinguishing features were his slightly popping eyes. He didn't look bored; he didn't look impatient; he didn't look patient. He looked as though waiting for someone was his job.

Big Six sat beside him, picking his teeth with a worn whalebone toothpick. He looked enormous in a bright-tan belted polo coat and wide-brimmed black velour hat pulled low over his eyes. His pockmarked face looked oversized; he had big gaps between big stained teeth.

A white drunk staggered past in the ankle-deep snow. A dark felt hat, mashed out of shape as though he had stepped on it in the snow, was stuck precariously on the back of his head. Thick, coarse, straight black hair was plastered back from a forehead as low as that of the Missing Link. The blue-white face with its beetle-brows, high cheekbones, coarse features, and wide, thin-lipped mouth looked part Indian. A dark blue overcoat smeared with snow on one side flagged open, showing a wrinkled, double-breasted, unstylish blue serge suit.

The drunk stopped suddenly, opened his trousers and began urinating on the right-front fender of the Cadillac, teetering back and forth.

Big Six opened the window and said, "Push off, mother-raper. Quit pissing on this car."

The drunk turned and peered at him through bloodshot black eyes. "I'll piss on you, black boy," he muttered in a Southern voice.

"I'm gonna see you do it," Big Six said, stuck the toothpick in his change pocket and opened the door.

"Let him go on," George Drake said. "Here comes Jackson down the stairs."

"I'm gonna flatten him is all," Big Six said. "Ain't gonna take a second."

In the right-side mirror, George noticed two colored men coming from beside the house in front of which he was parked. They were carrying battered Gladstone bags like Pullman porters on their way to work. They started across the street. The back window of the Cadillac was coated with snow, and he lost them in the rear-view mirror.

"Hurry up, man!" he called just as Big Six reached out a hand to clutch the drunk by the shoulder.

The drunk swung a long arc with his right hand, which he had held out of sight, and plunged the blade of a hunting knife through Big Six's head. It went in above the left temple, and two inches of the point came out on a direct line above the right temple. Big Six went deaf, dumb, and blind, but not unconscious. He teetered slightly and groped about aimlessly like an old blind man.

"Gooooodammmmm!" George Drake said, pushing open the

door with his left hand, while reaching inside of his coat for his pistol with his right.

He had his left foot down on the street, buried in the snow, and his left hand gripping the edge of the door for leverage, when a noose was dropped over his head and he was jerked backward. A knee caught him in the back, and he felt as though his spine was broken. His hat fell off. The sap landed right above his left ear, and lights exploded in his head as he lost consciousness.

"Put him in the back," the white man said from the other side of the car. "And put the keisters in the trunk."

He turned his head, gave a last look at Big Six and forgot him.

Big Six was walking slowly down the sidewalk, dragging his feet in the snow. The wound bled scarcely any; a thin trickle ran down his cheek from where the point of the knife protruded. His eyes were open; his hat was on his head. But for the bone knife-handle sticking from one temple and two inches of blade from the other, he looked like the usual drunk. He was calling silently for George to help him.

The white man got into the back of the car and took hold of the end of the noose. One of the colored men got behind the wheel; the other was at the back, putting away the Gladstone bags.

A shining black hearse backed carefully from the garage beside the funeral parlor. It straightened up and pulled to the curb. A fat black man in a dark chauffeur's uniform got out and closed the garage door. He looked across the street toward the Cadillac.

"Blink your lights once," the white man said from the rear.

The driver hit the bright lights for an instant.

Jackson waved his right hand and got into the hearse.

The snowplows hadn't got into the small side streets, and the hearse made slow progress until it came to Seventh Avenue. The Cadillac followed half a block behind with the lights dimmed.

The white man turned George Drake over on the floor, placed one foot on his back between the shoulder blades, the other on the back of his head, and drew the noose as tight as it would go. He kept it like that while the Cadillac followed down the cleaned traffic lane of Seventh Avenue and turned into 125th Street.

Scores of colored laborers, willing to pick up a few extra bucks on their off day, were shoveling the piles of snow into city dump trucks.

Cars were out again in the cleaned streets, and gay, laughing drunks were bar-hopping. Jokers were chunking tight, loose snowballs at their girl friends, who ran screaming in delight. A mail truck passed, emptying the boxes.

Big Six kept shuffling slowly toward Seventh Avenue with the knife stuck through his head. He passed a young couple. The woman gasped and turned ashy.

"It's a joke," the man said knowingly. "You can buy those things in the toy stores. Magical stuff. You stick 'em on each side of your head."

The woman shuddered. "It ain't funny," she said. "A big grown man like him playing with kid stuff."

He passed a woman with two children, on their way to the movies to see a horror film. The children shrieked. The woman was indignant.

"You ought to be ashamed of yourself, frightening little children," she accused.

Big Six kept on slowly, lost to the world. "George!" he was calling silently in the rational part of his mind. "George. The mother-raper stuck me."

He started across Seventh Avenue. Snow was banked against the curb, and his feet plowed into the snowbank. He slipped but somehow managed not to fall. He got into the traffic lane. He stepped in front of a fast-moving car. Brakes shrieked.

"Drunken idiot!" the driver cried. Then he saw the knife sticking from Big Six's head.

He jumped from his car, ran forward and took Big Six gently by the arm.

"My God in heaven," he said.

He was a young colored doctor doing his internship in Brooklyn Hospital. They had had a case similar to that a year ago; the other victim had been a colored man, also. The only way to save him was to leave the knife in the wound.

A woman started to get out of the car.

"Dick, can I help?" She had only seen the handle of the knife. She hadn't seen the blade coming out the other side.

"No—no, don't come near," he cautioned. "Drive to the first bar and telephone for an ambulance—better cross over to Small's; make a U-turn."

As she drove off, another car with two men stopped. "Need any help?" the driver called.

"Yeah, help me lay this man on the sidewalk. He's got a knife stuck through his head."

"Jumping Jesus!" the second occupant exclaimed, opening the far door to get out. "They think of new ways every day."

Cars were double-parked on Lexington Avenue in front of the hospital, and a large crowd of people milled about on the slushy sidewalks. Photographers and newsmen guarded the front door and the ambulance driveway looking sharply at everyone who left. Somehow word had got out that Casper Holmes was leaving the hospital, and they were determined he wouldn't get past.

Two prowl cars were parked across the street; uniformed cops stood about, beating their gloved hands together.

The heavy snow drifted down, leaving a mantle of white on hats and overcoats and umbrellas.

When the hearse drew up the cops cleared the entrance to the driveway.

A reporter opened the door of the driver's compartment and flashed a light into Jackson's face.

"It's just the chauffeur," he called over his shoulder to his colleagues; then he asked, "Who are you taking, Jack?"

"The late Mister Clefus Harper, a pneumonia victim," Jackson replied with a straight face.

"Anybody know a Clefus Harper?" the reporter asked.

No one knew him.

"Don't let me hold you up, Jack," he said.

The hearse purred slowly down the driveway toward the back exit.

"Keep on going," the white man in the rear of the Cadillac limousine said. "They're going to take a little time to get him out, and we got to get rid of this stiff."

The driver stepped it up, went past the double-parked cars and crossed 121st Street.

"Is he dead?" his companion asked.

"He ain't alive," the white man said as he bent over and began removing the noose from George Drake's neck.

When he had finished he began emptying all of Drake's pockets.

"Where we going to dump him?" the driver asked, as they approached 119th Street.

The white man looked about. He was not very familiar with Harlem.

"Turn down this street," he said. "It looks all right." The big car floundered in inches of snow.

"Can you get through to Third Avenue?" the white man asked.

"Sure," the driver said confidently. "A little snow like this won't stop a Cadillac."

The white man looked up and down the street. There was no one in sight. He opened the curb-side door.

"Pull in a little," he said.

The driver brushed the curb.

The white man rolled the body of George Drake out into the deep snow on the sidewalk. He closed the door and looked back once. The body looked like that of a fallen drunk, only there were no footsteps.

"Step it up," he said.

Jackson pulled up before the back door of the hospital from which the dead were removed. He was no stranger there.

He got out, went around, opened the back of the hearse and began dragging out a long wicker basket. Two grinning colored attendants came from within the hospital and took the wicker basket inside with them.

Jackson got back into the driver's seat and waited. He listened to an argument going on inside.

"You can't come back here and poke your nose into these dead baskets," an indignant voice was saying.

"Why not," a laconic voice replied. "It's a city hospital, ain't it?"

"I'll get the supervisor," the first voice threatened.

"All right, I'll go," the laconic voice acceded. "I wasn't looking for anyone; I was just curious as to how many people die in this joint during an average day."

"More than you think," the first voice said.

Eight minutes passed before the attendants reappeared, staggering beneath the weight of the loaded wicker basket. The lid was sealed with a metal clamp, to which was attached a name-card in a metal frame:

CLEFUS HARPER—male Negro
FOR: H. Exodus Clay Funeral Parlor
134th Street

They slid the basket into the coffin compartment and started to shut the doors.

"Let me do it," Jackson said.

The attendants grinned and re-entered the hospital.

"Where you want to go, Mister Holmes?" Jackson asked in a stage whisper.

"We're alone?" Casper asked in a low voice from within the basket.

"Yes, sir."

"Joe Green's boys are following in the Cadillac?"

"Yes, sir, they's waiting outside in the street."

"No one knows they're tailing us?"

"No, sir, not as far as I know of. They's keeping about a half a block behind."

"Okay. Then drive me to my office on 125th Street. You know where that is?"

"Yes, sir, up over the Paris Bar."

"Double-park somewhere close," Casper instructed. "Then get out and come back and open the basket. Then stand there as if you're doing something and watch the street. When it's safe for me to get out without being seen, give me the word. You got that?"

"Yessir."

"All right, let's go."

Jackson closed the back door and climbed back into the driver's seat. The hearse purred slowly up the driveway.

Before reaching the street it was stopped again by newspaper reporters. They looked at the name tag on the basket. One of them made a note of it. The others didn't bother.

The hearse turned toward 125th Street. Half a block distant it passed Joe Green's black Cadillac limousine. Jackson glanced at the Cadillac. It looked unoccupied. He began to worry. He drove slowly, watching it in his right-side fender mirror. When he had gone another half block, the Cadillac's bright lights blinked once and went off. He was relieved. He blinked his own lights in reply and kept driving slowly until he had made the turn into 125th Street and saw the black Cadillac make the turn half a block behind him.

He crossed Park, Madison, Lenox, keeping to the right, letting the fast traffic pass him.

At Seventh Avenue he waited for a snowplow to pass, pulled around a dump truck, parked in front of the clock, that was being loaded by a gang of well-liquored men. They stopped and watched the hearse cross the avenue.

"Somebody going by way of H. Clay," one of them remarked.

"Don't ask who it is," another replied. "It might be your mammy."

"Don't I know it," the first one replied.

A Cadillac limousine pulled around the truck in the wake of the hearse and carefully crossed the avenue.

"That's Joe Green's big Cat," a third laborer stated.

"Warn't his men in it," another replied.

"How you know? You running Joe's business?"

"Most generally he got George Drake driving and Big Six sitting in the front."

"Warn't Joe in the back, neither."

"Come on, you sports, and bend your backs," the truck driver said. "You ain't getting paid to second-guess Joe Green."

The hearse double-parked beside a Ford station wagon in front of the drugstore adjacent to the Paris Bar. The drugstore was open for business, and a few customers were moving about inside. The Paris Bar seemed crowded as usual. Its plate-glass windows were steamed over, and from within came the muted sound of a jump tune issuing from the juke box.

The Cadillac double-parked at the corner in front of the United Cigar Store.

Jackson got out on the driver's side, came around the front of the hearse and looked up and down the street. A couple of men issued from the Paris Bar, glanced at the hearse and went the other way.

Jackson went to the back, opened the doors and cut the metal seal on the wicker basket with his pocket knife.

Casper lay in the basket, fully dressed except for a hat. He wore the same dark clothes he had worn into the hospital. A soft black hat with the crown crushed in lay atop his stomach.

"Want me to help you up?" Jackson asked in a whisper.

"I can get up," Casper said roughly. "Close the doors and watch the street."

Jackson left the doors slightly ajar and looked one way and the other and then across the street. Cars passed in the street, a bus went by; people came and went along the sidewalks, trampling the deep snow into slush.

"Where's Joe's car parked?" Casper asked from the crack between the doors.

Jackson jumped. He wasn't used to people talking to him from the back of the hearse. He looked down the street and said, "In front of the Cigar Store."

"When you leave, give 'em a blink," Casper instructed. "How is it now?"

For a moment there was no one nearby; no one seemed to be looking in that direction.

"All right, if you come fast," Jackson said.

Casper came fast. He was down on the street in one jump, the black hat pulled low over his silver-white hair. He cleared the back end of the station wagon in two strides, leaped over the snow banked along the curb, slipped in the slush but caught himself, and the next instant was close to the doorway of the stairs leading to his offices above. His back was to the street as he inserted the key in the lock; no one had noticed him jump from the hearse; no one had recognized him; no one was paying him the least bit of attention. He got the door open and went inside, turned once and glanced at Jackson through the upper glass panel, signaled him to go on.

Jackson got back into the driver's seat, blinked his bright lights and looked into the rear-view mirror.

The Cadillac's bright lights blinked in reply.

The hearse drove slowly away.

The Cadillac pulled up and double-parked in the same position beside the station wagon.

"What you going to do with this heap?" the driver asked.

"Leave it right here, with the motor running," the white man said. "If Joe Green's a big shot, which he's gotta be, ain't nobody going to bother with it."

He took his short-barreled police special from his right overcoat pocket, held it in his lap and spun the chamber, then put it back into his pocket.

"I'll go first," he said.

He got out and crossed the sidewalk, side-stepped two men and a woman and tried the handle to the door.

The two colored men closed in behind him.

The handle turned; the door opened.

"He made it easy for us," the white man said, and started up the stairs, keeping close to the edges and walking on the balls of his feet.

The colored men followed.

"Lock the door behind you," the white man whispered over his shoulder.

18

Grave Digger and Coffin Ed sat in the car with the lights off on 19th Street, and waited. The motor was idling and the windshield wipers working.

Snow drifted down. The superintendents of the swank high-rent apartment houses flanking the private residences had their helpers out cleaning the sidewalks. Snowplows had already passed. The streets in this neighborhood were kept clean.

"I got a feeling we're missing something," Grave Digger lisped.

"Me, too," Coffin Ed agreed. "But we got to have somewhere to start."

"Maybe the sailor boy will hit it."

Coffin Ed looked at his watch.

"It's a quarter past seven. He's had ten minutes. If he hasn't hit it by now, he ain't never going to hit it."

"Blow for him, then."

Coffin Ed touched the horn, giving the prearranged signal. They watched in the rear-view mirrors.

Roman came out. Someone stood out of sight in the open door, watching him. He put his hat on the back of his head and started along the street.

When he came level, Grave Digger reached back, opened the door and said, "Get in."

A head came out of the open door, peered briefly and then withdrew. The door closed.

"What did you make out of it?" Coffin Ed asked.

"Whew!" Roman blew. A film of sweat shone on his smooth tan skin. "Nobody knew Mister Baron," he said. "Leastwise they all said they didn't." He blew again. "Jesus Godamighty!" he exclaimed. "Them people! And they's rich. And educated, too!"

"They knocked you out, eh?" Coffin Ed said absently.

He and Grave Digger stared at one another.

"We'd better stop by the hospital again," Coffin Ed suggested. He sounded dispirited and perplexed.

"We're losing time," Grave Digger said. "We had better phone."

Coffin Ed drove around Gramercy Square and stopped in front of a quiet, discreet-looking bar on Lexington. He got out and went inside.

Well-dressed white people were drinking aperitifs in a dim-lighted atmosphere of gold-lined wickedness. Coffin Ed fitted like Father Divine in the Vatican. He didn't let it bother him.

The bartender informed him with a blank face that they didn't have a phone. Bar customers on high stools looked at him covertly.

Coffin Ed flashed his shield. "Do that once more and you're out of business," he said.

Without a change of expression the bartender said, "In the rear to the right."

Coffin Ed restrained the impulse to yank him over the bar and hurried back to the telephone booth. A man was coming out; one was waiting to enter. Coffin Ed flashed his shield again and claimed priority.

He got the reception desk at the hospital.

"Mister Holmes is resting and cannot be disturbed," the cool voice said with a positive accent.

"This is Precinct Detective Edward Johnson on a matter of police business of an urgent nature," Coffin Ed said.

"I'll switch you to the supervisor," the reception nurse said.

The supervising nurse was patient and polite. She said that Mr. Holmes was not feeling well and could not for any reason be disturbed at that time; he had postponed his scheduled press conference until ten o'clock, and the doctor had given him a sedative.

"I can't say that I believe it, but what can I do?" Coffin Ed said angrily.

"Precisely," the supervisor said and hung up.

He phoned Casper's house. Mrs. Holmes answered. He identified himself. She waited.

"Have you been in contact with Casper?" he asked.

"Yes."

"When?"

"He telephoned this afternoon."

"Not during the past hour?"

"No."

"Might I ask when he is expected home?"

"He said that he will come home Tuesday evening—if there are no complications."

He thanked her, hung up and went back to the car.

"I don't like this," Grave Digger said.

Coffin Ed drove up Lexington Avenue, going fast, and turned over to Park Avenue at 35th Street, where the traffic moved faster. He skirted Grand Central Station on the upper ramp, skidding on the sharp corners and causing taxi drivers to shout at him.

"If I know Casper he'd get the hell out of that hospital as soon as he could," he half muttered as he accelerated up the slope toward 50th Street.

"Unless he's hiding," Grave Digger offered.

From the back seat Roman said, "If you-all are talking about Mister Holmes, he done already left the hospital."

The car slewed about and just missed a Lincoln limousine highballing in the middle lane. Coffin Ed pulled over to the curb, easing between two fast-moving cars, and parked at the corner of 51st Street. He joined Grave Digger in staring at Roman.

"Leastwise, that's what them people were saying in that house back there," Roman added defensively. "He'd phoned one of 'em from the hospital and said he'd be home by eight o'clock—one named Johnny."

"It's thirteen minutes to eight now," Coffin Ed said, looking at his watch. "I'd like to have that supervisor—"

"He fixed her; you know Casper," Grave Digger said absently.

They were both thinking hard.

"If you were Casper and you wanted to slip out, how would you do it?" Grave Digger asked.

"I ain't Casper, but I'd hire an ambulance."

"That's too obvious. The joint is crawling with newsmen, and, if anybody was laying for him, they'd spot it, too."

"A hearse," Coffin Ed suggested. "As many people as die in that hospital—"

"Clay!" Grave Digger said, cutting him off.

He looked about; the street was flanked with new skyscraper office buildings and a few remaining impregnable apartment houses.

"We got to get to a phone," he said, then added on sudden thought, "Drive over to the Seventeenth."

The 17th Precinct was on 51st Street, between Lexington and Third Avenues. They were there in two minutes.

Coffin Ed telephoned Clay with Grave Digger standing by. They had left Roman handcuffed in the car.

"Clay's burial home," came the old man's querulous voice.

"Clay. Ed Johnson and Digger Jones this end. Did you send a hearse to take Casper home?"

"I'm getting sick and tired of everybody wanting to guard the hearse I sent for Casper," the old man said tartly. "He already had Joe Green's boys—as if he couldn't take care of himself, mean as he is. And besides which he wanted it kept quiet. Then the Pinkertons sent men up—"

"What? The Pinkerton Agency?"

"That's what they told me. That they were sending three men on orders from—"

"Jesus Christ!" Coffin Ed said, breaking the connection. "Get the Pinkerton Detective Agency," he asked the switchboard operator.

When he had finished talking, he and Grave Digger looked at one another with as much fear in their eyes as either had ever seen.

"They no doubt got him by now—but why?" Coffin Ed said.

"That ain't the question now," Grave Digger lisped. "It's where?"

"There's got to be a tie-in," Coffin Ed said. "We've just missed it is all."

"We got one more card that we can play; we can make like we're a joker called Bernard Kaufman."

"We'd need to know his straight moniker."

"Makes no difference; we can play that one, since it's all we got to play," Grave Digger argued, "it might flush Baron into the open."

Coffin Ed began getting the idea. "You know, it might work at that," he conceded. "But we're going to need Roman's girl friend."

"Let's go get her, and let's hurry. We've just about ran out of time."

They went outside to their car and braced Roman.

"We're going to set a trap for Baron, son, and we're going to need your African queen to identify him," Coffin Ed said.

"I can't do that," Roman said. "You-all don't need her."

"We want you both, and there isn't any time to argue about it. A man's life might depend on this, a big man's life, an important man to us colored people any way you look at it—the way things are set up. If you help us now, we'll help you later. But if you don't we'll crucify you. Have you ever been cold?"

"Yes, sir, lots of times."

"But not as cold as we'll make you. We'll take you over to the river, handcuff your feet together, and let you hang in the water with all that snow they're dumping from the bridges."

Roman began to shiver just thinking about it.

Afterwards Coffin Ed admitted it might only have worked on an Alabama boy.

"If I tell you where she's at, you won't arrest her, will you?" Roman begged. "She ain't done nothing."

"If she helps us catch Baron, we'll decorate her," Coffin Ed promised.

They stood in the deserted office of the boathouse beside the lagoon, across from the apartment house in which Casper Holmes lived, using the telephone.

It was cold and damp; an inch-thick coating of ice covered the floor.

Coffin Ed was on the telephone, talking through the fine-tooth end of a gutta-percha comb held tight against the mouthpiece.

"This Bernie," he said. "Just listen, don't talk. There's a police tap on your line. Have Baron get in touch with me immediately."

"I don't know what you're talking about," a voice said coldly at the other end of the wire.

He hung up.

Grave Digger looked a question.

He shrugged.

Roman and Sassafras, standing to one side and handcuffed together, stared at him as though he had taken leave of his senses.

"If you is trying to imitate the Mister Bernard Kaufman, who stamped that bill of sale Mister Baron gave to Roman, you don't sound nothing like him," Sassafras said scornfully.

But the detectives had considered this.

"Well, let's go see if it works," Grave Digger lisped.

They took the handcuffed couple outside and crossed the sidewalk to Coffin Ed's Plymouth.

It was parked between two snow-covered cars of indistinguishable make, directly across 110th Street from the entrance to Casper's apartment house. Nothing about it indicated a police car.

Coffin Ed unlocked it, got in and started the motor and the windshield wipers. Grave Digger got into the front beside him; Roman and Sassafras piled into the back. Roman was still wearing his sailor suit; Sassafras wore the same ensemble she had the day before, with the exception of the red knitted cap, which she had exchanged for a green one.

Passing pedestrians, half-blinded by the snow, paid them no attention.

Sassafras leaned close to Roman and whispered conspiratorially, "I ain't heard yet from my friend."

She had been in hiding all day and hadn't learned that her friend with the experience had finally lost his head.

"But as soon as I do—"

"Hush your mouth!" Roman said tensely. "You ain't going to."

"Well, I like that!" she exclaimed indignantly and withdrew to the other side.

The Plymouth was pointed toward Fifth Avenue, which bounds Central Park on the east. All Fifth Avenue buses going north turned the corner into 110th Street and branched out toward their various destinations further on. The line's control office, where the schedules were checked and the personnel changed, was directly around the corner on the north side of 110th Street. Adjacent was a bar, facing the circular square, it contained the nearest public telephone.

Coffin Ed turned about on his seat and said, "Listen, we want you to watch the door across the street. If you see anyone come out that you know—anyone at all—tell us who it is."

"Yes, sir," they replied in unison and stared across the street.

A short, fat man came from the apartment. He was wearing a blue chesterfield overcoat, white scarf, and a black Homburg. Grave Digger looked from Roman to Sassafras. Neither showed any sign of recognition.

A middle-aged couple came out; a woman with a little girl went in; a tall man in a polo coat rushed out.

Leila Holmes came out. She was wearing dark slacks, black fur-lined boots, and a flowing ranch-mink coat. A wheat-colored cashmere scarf was wrapped about her head.

She began walking hurriedly toward the corner of Fifth Avenue.

Coffin Ed pushed the button for *drive* and eased the Plymouth out into the traffic lane. He drove ahead of the hurrying woman on the other side of the street and slowed down.

A streetlamp spilled a circle of white light on the white snow.

When Leila came into the circle of light, Sassafras exclaimed, "There's Mister Baron!"

Roman stiffened, leaned forward peering; his eyes popped. "Where?"

"Across the street!" Sassafras cried in her high keening voice. "In that fur coat! That's him!"

"That's a woman!" Roman shouted. "Has you gone crazy?"

"'Course he's a woman," Sassafras shrieked in an outraged voice. "I'd know that bitch anywhere."

Coffin Ed had already pulled ahead and was making a U-turn to head Leila off.

"Goddammit, girl, why didn't you tell me!" Roman raved in a popeyed fury.

"You think I was going to tell you he was a woman?" Sassafras said triumphantly.

The Plymouth had drawn abreast of Leila. Grave Digger got out, stepped over the snowbank and passed between two parked cars. Leila didn't see him until he took her by the arm.

Her face jerked up, tight with panic; her big brown eyes were pools of fear. Her smooth brown skin had turned powdery gray.

Then she recognized him. "Get your dirty hands off me, you stinking cop!" she screamed in a sudden rage and tried to jerk her arm free from his grip.

"Let's get into the car, *Mister* Baron," Grave Digger lisped in a cottony voice. "Or I'll slap you down right here in the street."

Blood surging to her face had given it the bright painted look of an Indian's. Her eyes had slitted like a cat's and glittered with animal fury. But she ceased to fight. She merely said in a strangled voice, "Play tough, buster; I'll have Casper break you for this."

"Casper ain't going to live that long, unless we find him quick," he lisped.

"Oh God!" she said with a moan and went limp.

He had practically to carry her to the waiting car. Coffin Ed opened the front door, and they installed her between them on the front seat.

"How did you make me?" she asked.

"It figures," Coffin Ed explained. "You had to be a woman or you'd be in the clique. And no one in the clique knew you."

"They only knew Casper," she said bitterly.

Grave Digger looked at his watch. "It's nineteen minutes past eight," he lisped. "Our only chance rides on how tough Casper is; and how much you're going to tell us; and how fast you're going to tell it."

She began to bristle. "I wasn't in with it, if that's what you think—"

"Save it," Coffin Ed grated.

"I just guessed it," she said. "I recognized the white man when they stopped us, after they'd run down Junior. I don't know why—"

"That can wait."

"I'd seen him talking to Casper Friday morning. I knew he was a stranger. Then I remembered Casper putting in a long-distance phone call to Indianapolis on Thursday night, right after he'd got the phone call from Grover Leighton. I wondered at the time what he was up to—"

Grave Digger exploded. "For chrissakes, get to the point!"

"Then when I found out they were the same ones who had robbed Casper, I knew he had hired them to do it." She took a deep breath, and her face twitched strangely. "Nobody could rob Casper unless he let them do it."

"It figures," Coffin Ed admitted.

"But why the snatch? What do they want with him now?"

She sighed. "He probably swung out on them."

"Double-crossed them?" Coffin Ed sounded slightly startled. "He'd double-cross these dangerous hoods?"

"Why not?" Leila said. "Casper would double-cross his own mother; and he's not scared of anybody who walks on two feet. He'd double-cross them and then job them. He probably had his brief case stuffed with newspapers when they pulled off that phony heist."

"They're going to kill him," Coffin Ed said.

"Not before they get the money," Grave Digger amended. "Where would he plant it?" he asked Leila.

"Somewhere in his office building," she said dully. "He didn't get to go anywhere else."

Grave Digger looked at his watch again. It was twenty-four minutes past eight.

The Plymouth was already rolling.

"Hold out, son," Grave Digger lisped in his cottony voice as he pulled his long-barreled, nickel-plated revolver from its shoulder sling and began checking the cartridges in the cylinder. "We're coming."

19

"Here goes nothing," Leila Baron Holmes said to herself.

She took a large ring of keys from her mink-coat pocket and began searching for the one that fitted the lock.

One side of her head and shoulders were highlighted in the upper glass panel by the red light of the neon sign from the Paris Bar next door.

In the pitch darkness at the head of the stairs, a man crouched, watching her. He shifted the .38 Colt automatic to his left hand, wiped his sweating right palm against his overcoat and renewed his grip on the butt. He sucked his bottom lip and waited.

Leila found the right key and got the door open. She returned the keys to her pocket and groped for the light switch on the wall to the right. Her gloved fingers touched it; she pushed the button, but no lights came on.

"Oh, damn!" she said in a tremulous voice that she had tried vainly to make sound annoyed.

She turned, locked the door behind her and began ascending the stairs. Her body was trembling from head to foot, and she had to force her reluctant feet to make each step.

A strong, nerve-tingling, aphrodisiacal scent of a French perfume preceded her.

The man at the top of the stairs drew back out of sight and waited.

When her foot touched the runner in the corridor, the man put his right forearm about her throat and his left elbow between her shoulder blades and lifted her from the floor, cutting off her wind.

She kicked and beat him futilely with her hands as he carried her down the corridor.

"Cut it out or I'll break your neck," he whispered thickly, blowing her perfumed hair out of his face.

She stopped fighting and began to squirm.

He stopped before the last door toward the front and kicked softly on the bottom panel.

The upper panel was frosted glass with the words:

Casper Holmes and Associates
Public Relations

spelled out in gold letters. But there was no light behind or in front, and the letters were a vague glittering.

The door opened inward abruptly. Nothing but the whites of the eyes of the man inside could be seen. The sound of Leila's strangled breathing was loud in the pregnant silence.

"What you got?" a whisper asked.

"A woman—can't you smell her?" the lookout whispered in reply, and stepped into Casper's reception room, still holding her suspended by the neck.

"What is it?" a Mississippi voice asked from the other room.

"A woman," the lookout repeated, unconsciously accenting the word.

Leila was rubbing herself seductively against him for all she was worth. Before arriving she had drenched herself in the aphrodisiacal perfume, and its scent, along with his own tongue swelling with lust, was choking him. Her trembling was setting him on fire. He lowered her to her feet and slackened his grip so she could breathe.

Suddenly a light came on in the private office, and the rectangle of a door appeared in the corner.

"Bring her in," the voice ordered.

The lookout pushed Leila through the doorway; the other man followed.

Her eyes widened in abject terror, and she moaned.

The office was a shambles. Drawers hung open, papers littered the floor, the leather upholstery was slashed, spare clothes from the closet were torn into shreds, the safe in one corner stood open.

A heavy green shade covered the window opening onto the inside airwell, and Venetian blinds were closed tightly over the two front windows.

Street sounds came faintly, muffled by the snow. There was the soft sound of snow falling into the airwell and water running in the drainpipes. No other sounds came from inside. They had the building to themselves.

Casper lay on his back on the dark maroon rug; his legs were spread-eagled, with his ankles lashed to the legs of the desk with halves of an extension cord. He was stripped to his underwear. His arms were twisted behind him so that his hands extended above his shoulder blades and were manacled with a set of handcuffs looped across his throat. He was gagged with his own black silk scarf, tightly twisted and passing through his mouth to a knot behind his head. Blood trickled from his eyelids, seeped steadily from his huge, flaring nostrils, ran from the corners of his mouth and flowed down his cheeks alongside the scarf that gagged him.

The desk lamp had been placed on the floor and focused into his face. It supplied the only light.

His eyes were closed, and he looked near death. But Leila knew intuitively that he was conscious and alert. The knowledge kept her from fainting, but it didn't help her terror.

The white man knelt beside him with a bloodstained knife pressed tightly against his throat. He had used the knife to slit Casper's eyelids and jab inside his nostrils and slash his tongue, and he had threatened to use it next to relieve him of his manhood.

His coarse black hair was still plastered to his head, but his nostrils had whitened at the corners. He stared at Leila from black eyes that had the bright enameled look of a snake's.

"Who's she?" he asked as though without interest.

"I don't know, she came up here with her own key."

"I'm Leila Holmes," she said in a voice that sounded as though her tongue had stuck to her teeth.

"Casper's whore," the white man said, getting to his feet. "Hold her, I'll stab her."

Leila whimpered and pushed closer to the lookout for protection. "You're not going to let that cracker hurt me," she begged in a tiny terror-stricken voice.

Suddenly, there was a horse of another color.

The black lookout shoved her to one side and drew his .38 automatic. He didn't aim it at the white man, but he showed it to him.

"I ain't going for that," he muttered.

The white man looked at him without expression.

"Go back and keep watch," he ordered.

"Door's locked," the lookout said.

"Go back anyway."

The lookout didn't move. "What you going to do with her?"

"Kill her, goddammit, what you think?" the white man said flatly. "You think I'm going to let her live and send me to the chair?"

"We can use her to make him talk," the lookout argued.

"You think he's going to talk to save this whore?"

Leila had inched over to the partition separating the two rooms and now began edging slowly toward the inside window.

"Don't let him kill me," she begged in her little-girl's voice to keep their attention distracted.

Her mouth was open; the tip of her tongue slid across her dry lips to make the red paint glisten. She stuck out her breasts and made her body sway as though her pelvic girdle was equipped with roller bearings. She was playing her sex along with her race for all it was worth; but her big brown eyes were dark pools of terror.

The white man turned his back on the lookout and moved toward her with the knife held in a stabbing position.

The second colored man said, "Wait a minute; he's going to shoot you."

The white man halted but kept staring at Leila without turning around. "What's the matter with you niggers?" he said. "The bitch has got to be silenced; and we ain't got all night to fool around."

The word *nigger* estranged him. Where before they were divided by a woman, now they were separated by race. Neither of the colored men moved or spoke.

Down below in the Paris Bar someone had put a coin in the juke box, and the slow hypnotic beat of an oldtime platter called *Bottom Blues* came faintly through the floor.

The second colored man decided to act as peacemaker. "Ain't no need of you two falling out about a woman," he said. "Let's consider it."

"Consider what?" the white man said. His big, sloping shoulders beneath the loose blue coat seemed suspended in motion.

Moving inch by inch, Leila played the lookout with eyes that promised a thousand nights of frenzied love. All of her life she had played sex for kicks; now she was playing it for her life and it didn't work the same; she felt as sexless as a leg of veal. But everything depended on it, and she forced words through her numb trembling lips.

"Don't let him kill me, please, I beg of you. I'll give you money—all the money you want. I'll be every kind of woman you can think of; just don't let him—"

"Shut up, whore," the white man said.

"Let's talk it over," the lookout mouthed. Lust was shaking him like electric shocks, half choking him, draining his stomach down into his groin.

"We've talked too much already," the white man said, moving into Leila and raising the knife.

Leila's hand flew to her mouth but she didn't dare scream.

The lookout moved forward and stuck the gun muzzle against

the small of the white man's back, then pulled it back a few inches so it could breathe; it was an automatic, and if he had to shoot it needed air.

The white man got the message. He froze with his hand raised. "You ain't going to shoot me," he said. His voice sounded as dangerous as a rattlesnake's warning.

"Just don't hurt her is all," the lookout said in a voice that sounded equally as dangerous.

The second colored man drew his own .38 police special, holding it down beside him in his left hand.

"This is getting too tight for me," he said. "I got fifteen grand wrapped up in this deal myself, and if it gets blown away we're all going to go."

"Chicken feed," Leila whispered, holding the lookout with her eyes.

Sweat had filmed on her temples and upper lip; a vein in the left side of her throat was throbbing. She breathed as though she couldn't get enough air; her breasts in the jersey-silk pullover were rising and falling like bellows. She was playing a sex pot if there ever was one; but all she wanted in this world was to get to the window, and it seemed like ten thousand miles away.

Unseen by the lookout, the white man turned the knife in his hand and gripped the point.

"This bitch is going to scream any minute," he said.

The lookout made an offer. "I'll give you my share for her."

Leila edged closer to the window. "You won't lose," she promised.

Nobody spoke. In the silence the slow, hypnotic beat coming from below repeated itself endlessly, changing instruments for eight-bar solos.

"It's a deal," the white man said. "Now get back on the door."

"I'll stay here—let Lefty take the door."

Leila turned her back to the window and groped behind her for the shade. Her fingers found the drawstring.

"Kill him!" she screamed and jerked the string.

Everything happened at once.

The shade flew up and spun at the top in a sudden chopping sound like a runaway ratchet wheel.

Leila dropped toward the floor as the white man threw the knife. It caught her in the stomach and went in up to the hilt.

The lookout swung his automatic, searching for a target.

Glass shattered, and the room exploded with the big, hard, head-splitting roar of a high-powered .38 as Grave Digger, standing on the snow-covered fire escape, shot through the iron window grill and put two slugs less than an inch apart in the gunman's heart.

Simultaneously, two shots sounded from the corridor; metal broke and wood crashed, and cold air rushed into the room.

The left-handed gunman spun toward the connecting doorway and went through with his pistol down at his left hip in the Hollywood gunslinger's fashion. He ran into a brace of slugs and came reeling back with two sudden eyes in his forehead, his coat flapping in the hard percussion of sound.

With no expression whatsoever in his beetle-browed, brutal face, the white man drew from the shoulder. He was lightning fast.

But Grave Digger had already taken a bead on him with the long nickel-plated barrel resting on an iron crossbar. He put the first one in the white man's right arm, just above the elbow, and the second one in his left kneecap.

The pistol dropped from the white man's hand as he pitched to the rug on his face. The pain in his knee was excruciating, but he didn't make a sound. He was like a wounded tiger, silent, crippled, but still as dangerous a killer as the jungle ever saw. Without looking up, knowing that he didn't have a chance, he turned over and lunged for his fallen pistol with his left hand.

Coffin Ed came in from the reception room and kicked it out of his reach, then crossed the room and shot the padlock off the window grill.

Grave Digger kicked it in, knocked out the broken window glass with the side of his shoe and came into the room. Snow followed him.

Leila was curled up against the baseboard with her hands gripping the handle of the knife, crying softly and moaning.

Grave Digger knelt down, pulled her hands away gently and handcuffed them behind her back.

"You can't pull it out," he said. "That would only kill you."

Coffin Ed was occupied handcuffing the white man's good left hand to his good right leg. The white man looked at him without expression.

Finally Casper opened his eyes. The scene was stained red by the blood on his eyeballs.

Coffin Ed undid the gag.

"Get me loose quick," Casper said thickly, talking through a mouthful of blood.

Grave Digger unlocked the manacles and Coffin Ed freed his legs.

Casper got to his hands and knees and looked about. He saw the manacled white man. Their gazes met. Casper saw the white man's revolver on the floor beside the desk. He crawled to it bear fashion and picked it up. Everyone was watching him, but no one except the white man expected it. He pumped three slugs into the white man's head.

Coffin Ed went crazy with rage. He kicked the pistol from Casper's hand and aimed his own revolver at Casper's heart.

"God-damned sonofabitch, I'll kill you!" he raved. "He was ours; he wasn't yours. You God-damned sonofabitch, we worked all night and all day and took every God-damned rape-fiend risk to get this hoodlum, and you kill him."

"It was self-defense," Casper said thickly, blood spattering from his slashed tongue. "You saw the mother-raper trying to shoot me—didn't you!"

Coffin Ed drew back his pistol as though to club him across the head. "I ought to knock out your God-damned brains and call it an accident," he raved.

"Easy, Ed, easy man," Grave Digger cautioned. "You ain't God, either."

Leila was laughing hysterically. "You knew what kind of man he is when you were risking me and everybody else to save him."

Grave Digger watched Casper pull to his feet and stagger toward the closet for some clothes to put on.

"Man, does money mean that much to you?" he asked.

"What money?" Casper said.

Down below on 125th Street was a crowd scene. Traffic was stopped. Joe Green's big black Cadillac limousine sat in a line of cars a block long, the motor running and nobody in it. The sidewalks on both sides of the street were jammed. The Paris Bar and the Palm Café and the Apollo Bar had erupted their clients. The three movie houses had been deserted for the bigger attraction.

"Gawwwaheddamnnnn. A shooting every night," a joker crowed triumphantly. "It's crazy, man, crazy."

Prowl cars converged from all directions, weaving in and out of the stopped cars, on the right side and on the wrong side of the street, jumping the curb when necessary to get by. Their sirens were screaming like the souls of the damned; their red lights were blinking like eyes from hell.

Cops jumped out, big feet splattering in the ankle-deep slush, went up the stairs like the introduction to the television series called *Gang Busters*.

Their eyes popped at the sight that greeted them.

Coffin Ed was telephoning for an ambulance.

Grave Digger looked up from the floor, where he was kneeling beside Leila Baron, stroking her forehead and consoling her.

"It's all over but the lying," he lisped.

20

Casper Holmes was back in the hospital.

His eyes and mouth were bandaged; he could not see nor talk. There were tubes up his nostrils, and he had been given enough morphine to knock out a junkie.

But he was still conscious and alert. There was nothing wrong with his ears, and he could write blind.

He was still playing God.

At eleven o'clock that night he held the press conference, which he had last scheduled for ten o'clock, against the considered advice of the staff doctors and his own private physician.

His room was packed with reporters and photographers. His chin jutted aggressively. His hands were expressive. He was in his métier.

He had scribbled a statement to the effect that the robbers had evidently been tipped off that he had received another payroll and had attempted a second robbery before getting out of town.

He had equipped himself with a small scratch pad and stylo with which to answer questions.

The questions came hard and fast.

He scribbled the answers, ripped off the pages and flung them toward the foot of the bed.

Question: Were you given a second payoff?

Answer: Hell no.

Question: Where did they get the information?

Answer: Ask a Ouija board.

Question: How did they find out about the first payoff?

Answer: Can't say.

Question: Why did you slip out of the hospital in a hearse?

Answer: Safety first.

Question: Why did you stop by your office?

Answer: Private reasons.

Question: How did it happen your wife was there?

Answer: I asked her to meet me.

Question: How did detectives Jones and Johnson locate you?

Answer: Ask them.

Question: How do you feel about it all?

Answer: Lucky.

So it went. He didn't give away a thing.

Afterwards he held a private session with his colored attorney, Frederick Douglas Henderson. He scribbled some instructions:

Get charges against sailor Roman Hill nol-prossed, give him your check for his $6,500 and get him out the country on first ship leaving. Then file claim in his name for the $6,500 found on the white robber's body. Then I want you to phone Clay and tell him to keep effects of body for me personally. Got all that?

Attorney Henderson read the instructions thoughtfully.

"Whose body?" he asked.

Casper wrote: He'll know.

When he left, Casper scribbled across a page: Keep your lip buttoned up.

He rang for the nurse and wrote: Get me an envelope.

She returned with the envelope. He folded the note, put it into the envelope and sealed it. He wrote across the face: Mrs. Casper Holmes. He handed it to the nurse.

Leila was in the adjoining room, but the nurse did not deliver the note.

She had been in an oxygen tent, taking plasma transfusions, ever since the operation. It was touch-and-go.

Big Six was in another smaller, cheaper private room, which was being paid for by Joe Green.

He had lapsed into a coma. The knife was still in his head. Orders were to leave it there until an encystment had formed about it in the brain, permitting its removal to be attempted. There was no record of such an operation being successful, and brain specialists all over the country had been alerted to the case.

George Drake's body was found shortly after midnight by a waiter on his way home from work.

He was the eighth victim taken to the morgue from Harlem that weekend resulting from what later became known as the Casper caper.

Grave Digger and Coffin Ed worked all night in the precinct station, writing their report. They stuck to the bare unadorned facts, omitting all references to Casper's private affairs and domestic life. Nevertheless, it filled fourteen sheets of foolscap paper.

It snowed all night, and Monday morning there was no letup in sight. The big suction-type snow removers had been put into use at midnight, and the city's snow crews had worked unceasingly in a slowly losing race against the snow.

At eleven o'clock that morning Roman Hill shipped out on a cargo vessel bound for Rio de Janeiro. He put $6,500 in cash in the captain's keeping before going to work.

Sassafras saw him off. As she was leaving the docks she met a man who reminded her of him very much. The man had a room in Brooklyn and invited her to a bar nearby to have a drink. She saw no reason why she should go all the way back to Harlem in that snow when you could find the same things in Brooklyn while the snow lasted.

At five minutes before noon two detectives from the Automobile Squad made a strike. They located the golden Cadillac in the showroom of a Cadillac dealer on midtown Broadway. It had been sitting outside the entrance to the service department, covered with snow, when the mechanics had shown up for work that morning.

No one admitted knowing how it had got there. It had been inside with the other demonstrator models when everybody left, and the place was locked eight o'clock Saturday evening.

One of the company's oldest salesmen, Herman Rose, closely resembled the description that Roman Hill had given of the man posing as Bernard Kaufman, who had notarized the phony bill of sale Mister Baron had given him.

But there were no charges against him and no one to identify him, so nothing could be done.

Grave Digger and Coffin Ed were summoned to the chief inspector's office in the headquarters building on Centre Street shortly after lunch.

The office was filled with brass, including an assistant D.A. and a special investigator from the commissioner's office.

They had been asked why they had attempted to apprehend the robbers single-handed, using Mrs. Holmes as a front, instead of contacting their precinct station and getting instructions from the officer in charge.

"We were trying to save his life," Coffin Ed replied. "If the block had been surrounded by police, those hoods would have killed him for sure."

The chief inspector nodded. It was a straw-man question anyway.

What the Brass really wanted was their opinion as to Casper's guilt.

"Who knows?" Grave Digger lisped.

"It hasn't been proven," Coffin Ed said. "All we know is what his wife said she guessed."

"What was her racket?" the chief inspector asked.

"We haven't figured it out," Coffin Ed admitted. "We got wound up in this other business and we haven't worked on it."

The chief inspector admitted that a crew of detectives from the Safe, Loft and Truck Squad and two experts from the Pinkerton Detective Agency had searched Casper's office and the entire office building, and had questioned all of the other tenants and the building superintendent. But they had not turned up the $50,000.

"You men know Harlem, and you know Holmes," the chief said. "Where would he hide it?"

"If he's got it," Grave Digger lisped.

"That's the fifty-thousand-dollar question," Coffin Ed said.

"All that I have to say about this business," the assistant D.A. said, "is that it stinks."

Now it was Monday night.

The snow crews had lost the race. The city was snowed in.

The customary metropolitan roar was muffled to an eerie silence by sixteen inches of snow.

Grave Digger and Coffin Ed were in the captain's office in the Harlem precinct station, talking over the case with their friend and superior officer, Lieutenant Anderson.

Grave Digger sat with one ham perched on the edge of the captain's desk, while Coffin Ed leaned against a corner radiator in the shadow.

"We know he did it," Grave Digger lisped. "But what can you do?"

Veins throbbed in Anderson's temples, and his pale-blue eyes looked remote.

"How did you figure the tie-in between Baron's racket and Casper's caper?" Anderson asked.

Grave Digger chuckled.

"It was easy," Coffin Ed said. "There wasn't any."

"We were just lucky," Grave Digger admitted. "It was just like she said; she guessed it."

"But you uncovered her," Anderson said.

"That's where we were lucky," Coffin Ed replied.

"What was her racket?"

"Maybe we'll never know for sure, but we figure it like this," Coffin Ed explained. "Leila Baron knew this salesman, Herman Rose. Casper bought his Cadillac from there. When she met Roman and found out he had saved up sixty-five hundred dollars to buy a car, she got Rose to come in with her and Junior Ball—or Black Beauty if you want to call him that—on a deal to trim him. Rose provided the car; he probably has a key to the place; he's been there long enough, and he's trusted. And he also acted as notary public. Then his part was finished. Baron was going to take Roman down that deserted street where Black Beauty, masquerading as an old woman, was going to fake being hit. They had no doubt worked out some way to get the car back from Roman and keep the money, too; we'll never know exactly unless she tells us. Probably she planned to scare him into leaving the country.

"Anyway, these hoods masqueraded as cops turned into the street as they were making their own getaway in time to see the whole play. They saw the Cadillac knock the old woman down; they saw the old woman getting up. They knew immediately it was a racket, and they decided on the spur of the moment to use it for their own purposes. They could get another car, which wouldn't be reported as stolen, and pick up some additional money, too. So they hit the phony victim deliberately to kill."

"They wouldn't have had to do that," Anderson said. "They could have got the Cadillac and the money anyway."

"They were playing it safe. With the phony victim really killed, no one could go to the police. They could use the Cadillac as long as they wanted without fear of being picked up."

"Vicious sonsofbitches," Anderson muttered.

"That was how we got the idea that the cases were connected," Grave Digger said. "There was an extraordinary viciousness about both capers."

"But why did they take the car back to the dealer's?" Anderson wondered.

"It was the safest thing to do when they finished with it," Coffin Ed contended. "The dealer's name and address were on a sticker in the rear window. Roman and his girl just didn't notice it."

Anderson sat for a time, musing.

"And you don't think his wife was connected in any way with his caper?" he asked.

"It doesn't figure," Grave Digger said. "She hates him."

"She'd have tipped the police if she had known about it in advance," Coffin Ed added.

"She tried to give us a lead, but we didn't pick it up," Grave Digger admitted. "When she sent us down to Zog Ziegler's crib. She figured that somebody down there would probably know about it, and we could find it out without her telling us."

"But we figured she was tipping us on Baron, and we missed it," Coffin Ed said.

"But she helped you to save him in the end," Anderson said. "How do you figure that?"

"She didn't want him taken by those hoodlums who had knocked her out and robbed her," Grave Digger said.

"Besides, she might still think Casper is a great man," Coffin Ed said.

"He is a great man," Grave Digger said. "According to our standards."

Anderson took his pipe from his side coat pocket and cleaned it with a small penknife over a report sheet. He filled it from an oilskin pouch and struck a kitchen match on the underside of the desk. When he had the pipe going, he said:

"I can understand Casper pulling off a caper like that. He probably wouldn't even think he was hurting anybody if he got away with it. The only people who'd get hurt would be some out-of-town hoods. But why would his wife get mixed up in a cheap chiseling racket like that? She's a lovely woman, a socialite. She had a hundred activities to keep her occupied."

"Hell, the reason is obvious," Coffin Ed said. "If you were a woman and you had a husband who played about with the little boys, what would you do?"

Anderson turned bright red.

Several minutes passed. No one said anything.

"You can hear your own thoughts moving around in this silence," Coffin Ed said.

"It's like an armistice, when the guns stop shooting," Anderson said.

"Let's hope we don't have to go through that again," Grave Digger said.

"What I have been thinking about is why Casper went by his office when it's obvious by now that he doesn't have the money hidden there," Anderson said.

"That's the big question," Coffin Ed admitted.

They brooded over it in the eerie silence.

"Maybe to throw off the Pinkertons who were on to him by then, or maybe to set a trap for the hoods if they were still in town. It was a red herring, anyway."

"Yeah," Grave Digger said. "We're missing something."

"Just like we missed that tip-off on Ziegler."

Grave Digger screwed about and looked at Coffin Ed.

"Yeah, maybe we're missing the same thing."

"You know what it is?" Coffin Ed said.

"Yeah, it just now came to me."

"Me, too. It was thinking about the clique that did it."

"Yeah, it's as obvious as the nose on your face."

"That's the trouble. It's too God-damned obvious."

"What are you two talking about?" Anderson asked.

"We'll tell you about it later," Coffin Ed said.

There was no way to drive down 134th Street.

Grave Digger and Coffin Ed left the Plymouth on Seventh Avenue, which had been kept open for the interstate trucks, and waded through snow that came up to their knees.

Mr. Clay was lying on his side on an old couch covered with faded gray velvet in the first-floor front room that he used for an office. His face was toward the wall and his back was toward the street of falling snow, but he was not asleep.

The dark-shaded floor lamp in the window that he kept lit permanently threw the room in dim relief.

He was a small, dried-up old man with parchment-like skin,

washed-out brown eyes, and long, bushy gray hair. As was customary, he was dressed in a frock coat, black-and-gray striped morning pants, and old-fashioned black patent-leather shoes with high-button, gray-suede leather tops. He wore a wing collar and a black silk ascot tie held in place by a gray pearl stickpin. Pince-nez glasses, attached to a long black ribbon pinned to the lapel of his coat, were tucked into a pocket of his gray double-breasted vest.

When Grave Digger and Coffin Ed walked into the office, he said without moving, "Is that you, Marcus?"

"It's Ed Johnson and Digger Jones," Coffin Ed said.

Mr. Clay turned over, swung his feet to the floor and sat up. He clipped the pince-nez onto his nose and looked at them.

"Don't shake the snow on my floor," he said in his thin, querulous voice. "Why didn't you clean yourselves outside."

"A little water won't hurt this place," Grave Digger lisped. "It'll help settle all this dust in here."

Mr. Clay looked at his swollen mouth. "Hah, somebody gave it to you this time," he said.

"I can't always be lucky," Grave Digger replied.

"Hot as you got it in here, you must be making mummies," Coffin Ed observed.

"You didn't come here to complain about the heat," Mr. Clay snapped.

"No, we came to examine the effects of a body you got in here."

"Whose body?"

"Lucius Lambert."

Mr. Clay refused flatly. "You can't see them."

"Why not?"

"Casper doesn't want them disturbed."

"Did Casper claim his body from the morgue?"

"A relative claimed him, but Casper is paying for the funeral."

"That don't give him any legal rights," Coffin Ed said. "We'll get an order from the relative. Who is he?"

"I don't have to tell you," Mr. Clay said peevishly.

"Naw, but you're going to have to do one or the other," Grave Digger lisped. "You can't hold bodies here without the proper authority."

"What did you want with his effects?"

"We just want to look at them. You can come with us if you want."

"I don't want to look at them; I've seen them. I'll send Marcus with you." He raised his voice and called, "Marcus!"

A tall, light-skinned, loose-lipped man affecting the latest English fashion came into the room. He was the embalmer.

"Show these dicks Lambert's effects," Mr. Clay directed. "And see that they don't take anything."

"Yes, sir," Marcus said.

He took them to a basement storeroom, adjacent to the embalming room, where the clothes and effects of the bodies were kept in small wicker baskets until claimed by relatives.

Marcus took one of the baskets from a shelf and placed it on the table.

"Help yourself," he said, and started from the room. At the door he turned and winked. "There's nothing in it worth taking, except a box of stockings, and the old man has already spotted them," he said.

"I'll bet you know," Coffin Ed said.

It didn't take but a few moments. Grave Digger pushed the clothes aside until he found the box of stockings.

It was a black box with a gold stripe across it, intended for twelve pairs of stockings. It was sealed with a tiny bit of Scotch tape.

Grave Digger peeled back the tape and removed two pairs of sheer silk stockings wrapped separately in gold cellophane paper. Underneath was another package wrapped in similar paper. He placed the package on the table and opened it.

It contained fifty brand-new thousand-dollar bills.

"It had to be," he said. "Snake Hips was the only one he could have passed it to. And we missed it all this time."

"It was right there in front of our eyes," Coffin Ed admitted.

"This boy would never have been dancing in the street half dressed on a night as cold as Saturday just to bitch off that square bartender. We ought to have known that."

"And he was in the clique, too. That's how we should have known. Casper passed him the package as he went by."

"Why do you think he left it here, Digger?"

"Safer here than anywhere else, and he probably didn't figure us to dig Snake Hips' straight moniker as Lucius Lambert."

"What are we going to do with it?"

"Let's just seal up this package and put it back and don't say anything about it," Grave Digger said.

"And keep the money?"

"Damn right keep the money."

"Casper's going to know we got it."

"Damn right he's going to know we got it. And there ain't going to be a damn thing he can do about it. That's what's going to hurt him. He's going to want to job us, but you can't job two detectives with twenty-five thousand bucks in their kicks. And as much as we know about him now, he knows he'd better not try."

"I'd like to see his face when he comes for it," Coffin Ed said.

"Yeah, there's going to be some arteries bursting for sure."

Two days later, the New York Herald Tribune Fresh Air Fund, which sends New York City boys of all races and creeds on vacations in the country during the summer, received an anonymous cash donation of $50,000. The executives of the fund didn't bat an eye; they were used to this kind of money.

On the same day, as he was about to leave the hospital, Casper received an anonymous telegram.

It read: *Crime doesn't pay.*

ALSO BY

Chester Himes

THE BIG GOLD DREAM

Alberta Wright drops dead on the street during a sermon by the charismatic con man Sweet Prophet. Her partner rushes home to avoid the cops, only to find her apartment looted by someone looking for her stash of cash. But soon it becomes apparent that there are a number of players in the race for Alberta's dough when a furniture salesman who bought most of her belongings is murdered at his shop. Coffin Ed Johnson and Grave Digger Jones are called in to investigate, but they know full well the bodies haven't stopped dropping yet.

Crime Fiction

BLIND MAN WITH A PISTOL

New York is sweltering in the summer heat, and Harlem is close to the boiling point. To Coffin Ed Johnson and Grave Digger Jones, at times it seems as if the whole world has gone mad. Trying, as always, to keep some kind of peace, Coffin Ed and Grave Digger find themselves pursuing two completely different cases through a maze of knifings, beatings, and riots that threaten to tear Harlem apart.

Crime Fiction

THE HEAT'S ON

From the start, nothing goes right for Coffin Ed and Grave Digger. They are disciplined for use of excessive force. Grave Digger is shot and his death announced in a hoax radio bulletin. Bodies pile up faster than Coffin Ed and Grave Digger can run. Yet, try as they might, they always seem to be one hot step behind the cause of all the mayhem—three million dollars' worth of heroin and a giant albino called Pinky.

Crime Fiction

COTTON COMES TO HARLEM

Flimflam man Deke O'Hara is no sooner out of Atlanta's state penitentiary than he's back on the streets working a big scam. As sponsor of the Back-to-Africa movement, he's counting on a big Harlem rally to produce a massive collection—for his own private charity. But the take is hijacked by white gunmen and hidden in a bale of cotton that suddenly everyone wants to get their hands on. As NYPD detectives Coffin Ed Johnson and Grave Digger Jones face the complexity of the scheme, we are treated to Himes's brand of hard-boiled crime fiction at its very best.

Crime Fiction

PLAN B

When acclaimed crime writer Chester Himes died in Spain in 1984, it was rumored that an unfinished story in the Harlem Detectives series existed that had all but extinguished his heroes and their fraught city in an explosive paroxysm of racial strife. Completed from his notes by Michel Fabre and Robert E. Skinner, *Plan B* is that harrowing story. The roots of racism and persecution in Tomsson Black's ancestry are deep and staggering. In his own lifetime, his misfortunes have become unbearable and, as they mount, serve as an impetus for a final and cataclysmic act of vengeance—the violent overthrow of white society.

Crime Fiction

ALSO AVAILABLE

The Crazy Kill
A Rage in Harlem
The Real Cool Killers